The Birth of Logan Station

The Birth of Logan Station

BILL BURCHARDT

DOUBLEDAY & COMPANY, INC.

GARDEN CITY, NEW YORK

1974

161 7091

Library of Congress Cataloging in Publication Data

Burchardt, Bill.
  The birth of Logan Station.

  I. Title.
PZ4.B9387Bi [PS3552.U494] 813'.5'4
ISBN 0-385-00519-9
Library of Congress Catalog Card Number: 74-6795

10-15-74 DD Western 2.50

The Birth of Logan Station

1

The Train, emptying itself of passengers, exuding the odors of its own iron sweat, stood in the huge train shed of the St. Louis depot disgorging luggage, baggage, and mail. A hiss of live steam blown from the boiler of the engine scalded the rock ballast of the track beneath it. The bell clanged restlessly.

Proceeding carefully among the clutter of baggage wagons plying the depot platform alongside the train, Lieutenant Britt Pierce, U.S.N., made his way toward the yawning maw of the concourse entrance. Traveling alone—always unsettling—his woolen uniform garb at odds with these surroundings, discomfitted him.

Shifting the seabag he lugged from right hand to left, he paused to purchase an evening St. Louis *Post-Dispatch* from a raucous newsie who shouted, "Casey gang suspected in Southwest City bank robbery! War in Oklahoma!"

Lieutenant Pierce snapped the paper into a double fold beneath his arm and again set his course dead ahead. His garb was strange for a man bound out across the American West. Black, laced shoes. Twin rows of gold buttons flared up his blue woolen uniform coat, and above its fold at the neck half an inch of starched white collar stood stiffly. Two broad gold stripes around each sleeve near the cuff indicated his rank.

The gold-embroidered star above the twin gold stripes, tarnished to bronze by salt sea water, indicated that he was a naval officer of the line. He was tall, lean, and youthful. His face was as brown as a walnut hull.

He continued through the crowd across the platform deck and

across the cobblestone concourse entrance. Here he paused, the seabag leaning against his leg, and surveyed the yawning, towering vastness of the depot.

In the tired human smell of the depot, acrid drafts of coal smoke swirled through in currents of air as doors swung and people hurried. With his sea chest already checked through to Kansas City on the Missouri-Pacific sleeper, it was a matter of where to pass the time.

Before him ranged the row of ticket wickets with their lines of waiting travelers. The curving counter of magazines, gimcracks, candy, and apples did not look inviting. Neither did the depot restaurant with its scatter of partly occupied tables, but there were unoccupied seats along the lunch counter.

He hoisted his seabag and proceeded. Sitting at the lunch counter he opened the newspaper. Its dateline read *St. Louis, Saturday, April 20, 1889.* A legend in tall type proclaimed WAR IN OKLAHOMA. A BLOODY BATTLE BETWEEN BOOMERS AND DEPUTY MARSHALS NEAR PURCELL.

With full interest, Pierce read the subhead: THE UNITED STATES DEPUTY MARSHALS PURSUE THE RAIDERS—FIERCE CONFLICT BETWEEN THE TWO FORCES.

> Purcell, Indian Territory—For several days men on horseback and in wagons have been seen fording the South Canadian, north of Purcell, and disappearing in the timber to the eastward. Men who come in from hunting trips reported having seen large bodies of boomers moving in a northeasterly direction, and a hunter who arrived last night declared that he had found a man in a secluded valley about twenty miles from Purcell. Yesterday morning at sunrise thirteen prairie schooners, well manned, crossed the Santa Fe tracks below the city and forded the river. The drivers urged their animals—

Movement behind the lunch counter drew Pierce's attention. A waitress had stationed herself before him. He drew his thoughts from the strangeness of the news story to the reality of the depot restaurant and ordered coffee.

Pierce looked around curiously. Traveling alone, sitting in a public place, he resented the feeling that always beset him. The feeling that people were watching him was plaguing. A self-conscious sense of aloneness drove his attention back to the newspaper for escape.

—and the train was across and out of sight before many of the residents of Purcell were stirring. A citizen saw them, however, and he acquainted others who have staked claims and hope to occupy them soon after noon on Monday next. The story soon gained general circulation and before noon a meeting was held. The feeling against the trespassers ran high and inside of thirty minutes a half dozen fiery speeches had been made. It was finally decided that the Chief Deputy Marshal be called upon to try to

Expel the Raiders.

In the afternoon the Chief Deputy, accompanied by thirteen assistants rode down to the river and took the same ford. There was a fresh trail leading to the northeast, and the party followed this at a gallop. About four miles out one of the men noticed a thin cloud of smoke rising—

His coffee came. Britt tasted it and the scalding heat of it was warming. His eyes sorted the scattering of travelers at nearby tables. A thought, *I'm the watcher, and not being watched,* mildly amused him for a moment, but did not make him comfortable in idly staring about the depot restaurant. Once more he dropped his attention to the newspaper.

—thin cloud of smoke rising above the cottonwoods to the right. A halt was called and three of the party reconnoitered. They discovered four wagons about three hundred feet from the trail and five men seated around a fire eating their dinner. These were unceremoniously ordered to hitch up. The enterprising boomers were thoroughly scared, and in less than fifteen minutes were on the back trail in charge of one of the deputies who was ordered to escort them across the river and then picket the fording places until his comrades returned. The latter deployed as skirmishers and advanced—

Penetrating his interest in the story he was reading, the sensation of being watched nettled Lieutenant Pierce even more strongly. He grimly denied it and continued down the newspaper column.

—advanced slowly several miles. Suddenly a shot was heard on the left, and a bullet clipped a leaf above the head of one of the party. A minute later a volley rang out in front, and the pony ridden by one of the deputies sank to the ground with a bullet in his head. The chief of the deputies called out for his men to charge. Each had unslung his Winchester.

Lieutenant Britt Pierce looked up, surveying the crowded short-order tables around him with careful thoroughness.

A short, squarely built, redheaded man, sitting alone at a near table, removed his gaze quickly to sit studying the polished marble tabletop. His cornering glance still flicked curiously toward Pierce from the edges of his eyes.

Pierce studied him in non-recognition and, frowning, flipped his newspaper into a new fold. He finished the account of the gun battle, reviewed the column thoughtfully, and read one more brief item.

BOOMERS MAKE A SNEAK

Kansas City, Mo., April 20—A special from Arkansas City says that it has been estimated by ranchmen that from five hundred to one thousand boomers will have an illicit entrance into Oklahoma before noon of the 22nd. These boomers generally strike west of the El Reno Trail toward the Cimarron and enter the western portion of the territory. The interest now centers in Logan Station. It is thought that by Tuesday there will be 10,000 people in and about the Station. The material for 500 houses has been shipped from one Chicago firm alone. The telegraph company is preparing for a tremendous day's business on Monday. It has been estimated that there will be 100,000 words of special dispatches from Oklahoma on the day of opening.

The story of a stagecoach robbery "between Watonga and Fort Reno on the borders of the Oklahoma country" drew his attention and he read it almost to its conclusion before the thought struck him with force.

This is intolerable, Britt decided. He looked up to find that the stubby redheaded man had risen and stood staring at him openly. Britt Pierce returned the stare. Their eyes locked, fixedly. Then a mellowing surprise softened Pierce's features, and he too stood up.

They eyed each other. Warmth grew in Pierce's face. He stepped forward, but when he spoke there was a touch of uncertainty in his friendly tone.

"Roody Andrews?" he asked doubtfully.

The man's pink complexion brightened with glee. His red hair had the appearance of being sewed to his hat like the fright wig of a stage comedian. Beneath the hair his ears wiggled. He poked Pierce with a short finger and exclaimed, "Britt Pierce! I couldn't be sure—with that monkey suit."

Resentment crossed Britt's face and he stiffened, "When there's a war on, we look great to you civilians. In peacetime you take us for zoo-keepers or hotel doormen."

The short man winked, his good humor bubbling and enthusiastic. His own checked suit was expensive. His waistcoat crosslapped generously. His cravat was of knitted silk, so darkly green it was nearly black, and thrust with a white pearl stickpin.

"Navy-blue serge." He fingered Britt's jacket sleeve. "Bet the seat of your pants is so shiny if you tore 'em you'd have seven years' bad luck."

"All right, Roody," Pierce yielded, "I surrender. I'll strike my flag."

"I'll remember to call you 'sir' to keep you from striking me," Roody punned. "How about a drink? The Market Street Saloon is just around the corner."

As they moved through the crowded waiting room Roody asked interestedly, "Where are you bound?"

"Los Angeles."

"Routed how?"

"Missouri-Pacific to Kansas City, Santa Fe to Albuquerque, A. & P. on to the Coast."

"Great." Roody reached up to put a friendly hand on Pierce's shoulder. "We'll be on the same train through to Wichita."

Andrews steered right at the cobblestone sidewalk. The pale spring sun of northern Missouri's April was slipping low on the cluttered St. Louis skyline. The air smelled damp, smoke-tainted, and sharply chill.

"I'm waiting for my sister," Roody said briskly. "She's coming in on the Wabash from St. Charles." Resentment seeped into his voice, "Her train's running half an hour late."

They entered the Market Street Saloon, a quiet bay at this dinner hour, and ordered whiskey. Roody Andrews grabbed Britt's reaching hand, "No, no. Keep your money. This one is on me."

They drank. A quiet lull filled the saloon. Britt put one black shoe on the brass rail and surveyed the length of the empty bar. A card game was in progress at the back of the room.

"You remember my sister?" Roody asked.

Pierce nodded thoughtfully. "The last time I saw her she was sitting on the levee, barefooted, playing a harmonica. That was, I expect, ten years ago."

Andrews' expression knotted with a small Irish anger. "She hasn't changed. Still carries that damned harmonica!"

Britt saw the scowl in the bar mirror. He glanced away to look at the glass window fronting the sidewalk. It was turning dark. The day was gone. At the back of the saloon, a card player stood to remove a glass globe, open the gas jet, and strike a match beside the gaslight mantle. The light flared, hissing softly. The player replaced the globe and rejoined the gamblers at the table, fanning his cards open in the glow of illumination.

Bemused, Britt sipped his whiskey. "Still goes barefooted?" he asked.

"Oh, no. She's twenty-one years old. I finally got shoes on her." The undertone of anger in Roody's voice could hardly be interpreted as joking. "Where have you been, Britt?"

Lieutenant Pierce grinned in amusement. "You mean recently? Or since I left Pittsburg Landing."

"Well, hell, in general." Roody eyed him closely. "I know you've been at sea. Your mug is too dark for this early spring. Fill me in. Not a complete biography, you know."

"Aye, aye, sir," Pierce said briskly. "Commissioned in '82. Six months duty aboard the steam sloop *Congress* in the Mediterranean. Back to New York to decommission the sloop, then aboard the frigate *Tennessee,* which hardly ever got out of the Navy yard. Finally got to sea again in the commissioning crew of the U.S.S. *Boston.* Most recent duty, a briefing by Captain Mahan at the Newport War College. That sketchy enough for you?"

"We're not that pressed for time." Roody's beckoning motion summoned the bartender.

Pierce turned his glass upside down on the bar, a gesture of which Roody sharply disapproved. "Come on," Roody insisted brusquely. "Just one more. I'm buying."

Britt shook his head, saying pleasantly, "That's my ration before supper."

"Well, tell me more while I drink mine," Roody lifted his glass. "A shot of Irish whiskey makes me feel half an inch taller."

"I'm at the bitter end of a thirty-day leave," Pierce said.

"Spent a couple weeks at the Landing—my mother still lives there. Came down the river on the *Delta Queen* to Cairo last week and caught the B.O. & Q. to St. Louis. I'm due in Los Angeles the end of the month."

A speculative thought began to form in Roody Andrews's pink features and he commented, "I noticed you were reading the newspaper."

"Yes"—Britt glanced at the newspaper he had laid on the bar—"quite an excitement between us and California."

Andrews reached to unfold the paper. "Being a Navy man," he suggested, "it would appear that this item would be of interest to you."

Roody's blunt thumb lay across a front-page column headed THE APIA DISASTER, Admiral Kimberly's Official Report to the Secretary of the Navy.

"Old news," Britt said grimly. "I had a letter from Admiral Porter while I was still at the Landing." He folded the newspaper shut. "What about you, Roody? What have you been at since we last ran a trotline?"

"That really would be dull news to an adventurer like you." Andrews drank off his whiskey. "I went in the banking business as soon as I finished law school. I'm vice-president of our branch in Kansas City now."

"I got the impression," Britt puzzled, "that you were just passing through Kansas City. You said—"

The shrewd speculation that had begun in Roody's eyes spread. He pursed his lips, glancing sharply at the scrolled, mahogany clock that hung with swinging pendulum beneath a spread of deer antlers at the rear of the saloon.

"Here," he said, "give me that newspaper. Here's an item you missed."

2

Roody Andrews spread the thin edition open on the bar, and turned to page seven. The stacked heads and banks drew down toward the story like the vortex of a whirlpool—

THE PROMISED LAND
*The Plains of Oklahoma Greet the Eyes of the
Boomers—Thousands of Men Along the Line
Ready for the Rush—Troops Guard the
Border but Plans are Laid to
Bribe the Guards and Pass
the Line Before the
Appointed Hour.*

The *Post-Dispatch* staff artist had been given free rein. Beside the opening initial letter, a frontier cavalryman galloped headlong with upraised campaign hat. A drawn map of the Indian Territory outlined the borders of the Oklahoma lands, with the town sites along the Santa Fe right of way: Wichita, Winfield, Arkansas City, and crossing the border into the Territory: Perry, Orlando, Logan Station.

A three-column sketch—*A Relay House on the Mail Route*— illustrated the log stagecoach station at Kingfisher, a four-horse Concord coach pulling away from it. A two-column illustration portrayed *The Business Street of Purcell, Indian Territory;* a row of false-fronted stores and saloons fronting a wide street through which a covered wagon moved and a pair of cowboys galloped in the opposite direction.

A single-column sketch depicted a granger wagon *Crossing*

the Canadian River, while a horseman, wearing a battered sombrero, neck scarf, and knee boots, paused to permit his horse to drink the shallow water near the bank.

Below, the artist had drawn the pitched tents of the *Camp of the 5th U. S. Cavalry at Logan Station*. A mounted black cavalryman, erect and soldierly, was illustrated cantering his horse between the row of tents and a supply wagon.

In the harsh voice of suppressed excitement, Roody Andrews read aloud: *"On the Oklahoma Line, April 19, by Courier via Arkansas City.*

*"*The boomers are in sight of their Eldorado at last. After a march of three days over the muddy trails of the Cherokee Strip, they halted at sundown within a hundred yards of the beautiful land of the Chickasaws. The first glimpse of a harbor light was never more welcome to a storm-tossed sailor"—Roody paused to glance meaningfully at Britt—"than were the rolling green plains to the hardy column of white-topped prairie schooners. They entered with cheers and volleys of musketry. Horsemen, who have accompanied the long procession as guides spurred their ponies forward and dashed in upon the soil which has been the happiest dream of their lives, but were promptly escorted back to the wagons by Captain Hayes' troopers and ordered to remain there until Monday.

"There are men on the line representing every element of wild western society. They ride the fleetest ponies in the Territory, and they are thoroughly acquainted with Oklahoma. They have an advantage over the homesteaders which can hardly be appreciated now. They are all armed to the teeth and are boasting that they will not tolerate rivalry or opposition. These men are bound to precipitate trouble."

Roody paused and glanced impatiently up at the clock above the saloon gaslight. "We'd better go," he said, irritated that he had to interrupt himself. "Evelyn's train should be in the depot by the time we get back."

Roody continued to read as they paced along beneath St.

Louis's street arc lights. "It is said that at exact noon Monday, when the signal will be fired, there will be no point on the line of the Oklahoma country that will not hear it. The patrol around the country will all shoot and no point on the boundary will be out of hearing. Some of the colonies have made arrangements to give one long yell as soon as the alarm is given, then start on the run. This plan, however, is ridiculed by those who say it will be best to yell after getting a claim rather than at the beginning of the run."

Roody Andrews read in dry-throated rush, as if he could not get enough of the printed account. Stumbling on an upthrust cobblestone in the walkway, he paused and stood halted dazedly.

"You've gone overboard, Roody," Britt frowned. "You're gulping this landrush melodrama like a bos'n's mate drinking beer. To leave the banking business and jump on a horse to run for a granger claim? Somehow, I can't see you in bib overalls farming—"

"No, no!" Roody burst out. "You didn't let me finish. I've got a charter to open a branch bank down there. My own bank. I'll be the president of the new Commercial Bank at Logan Station. And Logan Station is going to be the capital of the Territory!" Roody's eyes glowed hot with enthusiasm.

Britt studied Roody's excited, distant-focused gaze, knowing that the friend of his youth was envisioning a strange and yonderly mirage. Roody's face was flushed. "Come with me," he urged, seizing Britt's arm. "You've got time. It would just be a detour south from Wichita. It's going to be the wildest show since the New York draft riots. You owe yourself the pleasure. It'll give us a chance to rehash old times—"

"We can do that right now," Pierce said. "That look in your eyes reminds me of the time you decided to borrow Squire Nicholas's team of trotters."

Roody scowled, drawn from the future to probe the past. He muttered, "Oh? Yes—"

Britt took his arm, steering him on toward the Union Depot

entrance. "We were out for recess. Remember? Standing there in the schoolhouse yard, you saw the squire leave his buggy and that team of fast bays ground tied in front of the preacher's house."

Roody nodded, hurrying along the cobblestone walk. "I wanted you to go with me," he recalled.

"A good thing I didn't," Britt prodded grimly.

"Uh-huh." Roody's smile was guilty. "They ran away with me. If you hadn't been there in the schoolyard to run out and stop them—"

"I didn't stop them," Britt disagreed. "I was scared half-witted. All I did was run out and holler."

"Right in front of that run-away team!" Roody declared. "That stopped them until Nicholas could run out and grab them. Then the schoolmaster—"

"Yeah." Britt was rueful. "Then the schoolmaster!"

"What was his name?" Roody tried to remember.

"Griggs." Britt remembered all too clearly. "Professor Griggs."

"You got the whipping." Roody was obviously ashamed to remember. "He thought *you'd* spooked the team to run, and that I'd climbed in the buggy to try to stop them."

Roody stopped to stand thoughtfully. "I've thought about that a lot of times, Britt." He stood, short and embarrassed, on the walk. "I could have straightened that out. I was just plain yellow." He paused, then added roguishly, "And you were red, white, and blue. Old man Griggs sure could wield those canes, couldn't he?"

To Britt, it was not quite so funny. He remembered the pain and the shame of that undeserved hiding with no fondness. "Griggs could wield them," he agreed.

"Well, what's past is past." Roody dismissed it lightly. "I should have apologized to you a long time ago. But I'll make it up and more on this trip to Oklahoma Territory, Britt."

Beyond the depot the impatient blast of a steam whistle cut the air, replaced then by the bell clang of a train entering the railroad yard, and Britt suggested, "Shouldn't we get on back to the platform? Perhaps that's your sister's train."

Unable to break the grip of his own anticipation Roody turned to accompany Britt into the station. "Come with me, Britt," Roody urged once more. "You'll be treated royally."

"By who?"

"By me," Roody declared.

"Just like I was when you tried to coax me into that buggy-borrowing escapade," Britt nodded. "Roody, you're going into Oklahoma and right into trouble. I can see it in your eyes."

"Trouble!" Roody exploded. "What trouble? I've told you—"

Britt interrupted. "You told me you're vice-president of the—" He paused.

"The Commercial Bank of Kansas City," Roody said impatiently.

"All right," Britt tempered, "then why go to work for another bank, in rough country—"

"Money, man! Money!" Roody declared. "Thousands of new customers. A new town where there isn't any bank. And I'll be the bank's president."

"Could be you're greedy," Pierce speculated.

"Greedy, greedy, greedy." Roody's eyes glowed. He smiled greedily. "Damn right I'm greedy." His gaze turned fuzzy with distance again.

Britt said in half-serious demeanor, "I'd better go along—to take care of you."

They threaded the crowd toward the train shed. Roody shook the newspaper.

"There's a special train leaving Chicago tonight. Two hundred Oklahoma colonists on board. It's in the paper here. Another story tells about a one-armed veteran—what was his name—Edward Evans—striking out with a carload of tents. Going to start Logan Station's first hotel with them. His wife will be the cook. The Boomers—"

"I kept reading that word," Britt nodded. "What are Boomers?"

"All of us," Roody replied. "We've been booming Oklahoma for settlement. Nothing but Indian land down there. What's needed are white settlers!"

"And the Indians?"

"Shiftless," Roody decreed. "No ambition. Lazy. What's needed is organization. White men. Planning. Reap the harvests of that rich land. There's probably minerals there. The buffalo are gone. Indians have got to realize that! Time to change. Only the white man can change that land. No more buffalo. But the Boomers are coming." Roody smacked an open palm with the folded newspaper, thrusting it at Britt. "Here, read about it. Bigger crowd at the Union Depot this morning than when President Cleveland stopped here in the fall of '87. The paper says so. All of them bound for Oklahoma. Nearly every state east of the Mississippi represented. Men, women, children! Colonists! Boomers!"

As Britt and Roody moved out on the depot platform, gloomy now with night darkness above the high iron train shed, Roody's voice was lost in the clamor of the slow approaching locomotive. Britt could see Roody's lips moving although his voice was lost in the creak of the iron drivers cranking the engine's high wheels past. The engine cab crawled by, WABASH lettered tall and dimly white beneath the outleaning form of the engineer. Roody's face grew fiery in the red glint of light reflected from the train's roaring furnace, then the engine was gone by and they stood in dim gloom beside the squealing, creaking roll of dull black passenger coaches. In expiring groans, the train halted.

The red-haired young banker's eyes scanned along the line of cars. A pasty, ghostlike face pressed against the glass of the chair car beyond them sought attention with a wavering, drab-gloved hand.

"There's Aunt Lorna, waving from the window." Roody moved toward the chair car vestibule, edging into the descending passengers with the current of others moving to greet arrivals.

The ghostlike face disappeared from the chair car window.

It reappeared presently, atop the stocky body of a plainly dressed elderly woman who shrugged her shoulders into a dark gray shawl and seized the iron hand rail to descend from the train.

Roody's progress through the crowd was slow. His hat was raked askew as he passed a waving-armed female. Roody glared up in anger at the woman's gesturing arm. Britt watched Roody mouth sharply wrathy words as he smoothed his wig-like hair, squared his hat, and stepped to greet his aunt. She turned a sallow cheek to receive his peck.

The platform at the rear of the car emptied, further debarkation from the coach prevented by a fat brown-derbied drummer who stopped, blocking the chair car exit. The girl behind the fat man crowded herself into the door alongside him, rudely shoving him against the iron door frame. Cigar ashes cascaded down his vest as her elbow drilled his ribs. She was out then, like a cork popping out of a bottle, and at the stinging glance she turned back on him the fat man lifted his brown derby in mute apology. The girl came down the train's steps in quick jumps, lifting her skirt to leap the conductor's stool.

Britt observed her performance with growing amazement as she turned an aggressive shoulder to launch through the crowd toward Roody. She carried her purse loosely on her left arm. A roughly garbed youth approached her from the left and Britt recognized his purpose when he saw a knife blade flash open in the man's lifting hand.

A warning shout formed in Britt's throat and he shoved into the crowd in an effort to reach the girl before the young thug could act. His shout only confused the crowd and increased the resistance to his attempts to press through.

The rough-dressed youth took advantage of the confusion, gripping the edge of the girl's purse as he brought the edge of his knife against its carrying strap. She seemed suddenly aware of his presence then and her reaction was fast and flawless.

In swift motion her heel spiked his kneecap. Her forearm

boosted the knife-holding hand up before her face and she sank teeth in his wrist. The knife clattered to the wooden platform. The shaggy-haired young thug went down clutching his knee with a grimace of pain. But the girl was not through and she hoisted her skirt and cocked a kicking foot. Roody Andrews shoved past to confront her.

"Evelyn!" he shouted. "What in the hell are you doing?"

Britt reached to grasp Roody's arm.

"It's all right, Roody," Britt said firmly. "I saw it. The fellow tried—"

The girl's voice was bitter as she said to the cowering man, "Get up from there, you —— — — ——!"

It was an epithet Britt Pierce had heard from many a bos'n's mate, but never from so ladylike a young woman. It silenced him and brought the milling, surrounding crowd to silent attention.

The girl stood taut, grim, not unpretty, trimly made and petite, and Britt Pierce felt a pang of sudden interest in her. It was as sharp and tangy as a bee sting. Like the tart-wine spice of biting a hard red apple. There was no ignoring the feeling and it momentarily awed him.

She looked down at the fallen man as if scornfully dismissing him from existence. "Then lay there and rot, damn you," she said and stepped back. A helmeted policeman came levering his way with billy club and bull-necked determination through the circle of onlookers.

3

The thief, seeing the coming policeman, struggled up and limped off into the crowd. The policeman pursued him.

Roody began shoving his sister and aunt away in the opposite direction. Britt, uncertain as to what he should do, followed, moving slowly through the milling spectators. Roody hurried the girl and her aunt, firmly holding the elbow of each, until he found seclusion behind a laden freight wagon on the depot platform.

He turned then and Britt could see that he was scowling ominously. As Britt came near Roody sighed, a despairing rush of outblown breath, and released his sister's arm. He spoke to the older woman.

"Aunt Lorna"—Roody was grimly polite—"I'd like to present my old friend Lieutenant Britt Pierce of the U. S. Navy. We were boys together at Pittsburg Landing."

Aunt Lorna, a dumpy bittern whose dry-apple face was immune to the emotions of this world, ignored the hullabaloo eddying around her. She stood haughtily aside and gave a nod of recognition toward Britt.

"Britt, you remember my sister Evelyn." Roody sighed again.

Britt removed his visored cap with its tarnished insignia of crossed gold anchors and U.S.N. shield. "At your service, ladies."

His voice drew Evelyn Andrews' attention. Her gaze turned up to him with some intensity. "Yes," she said, "I think I remember you."

Britt suspected that Aunt Lorna had a low regard for Yankee

officers. On her mounded bosom a United Daughters of the Confederacy pin rode proudly.

Roody's sister stepped directly in front of Britt, standing close, looking up at him. She said in lively fashion, "I'm called Eve."

With a sense of excitement Britt stood motionless, his cap held between himself and the girl. Roody Andrews reached for his sister's arm and drew her back with another sighing exhalation of despair.

"Aunt Lorna," Roody said, "I surely appreciate your bringing Evelyn down."

Aunt Lorna, in absent hauteur, nodded. "Young girls should never travel alone."

Roody grumbled, "Neither should any wild creature from which people should be protected."

A train-caller's droning announcement drifted down the platform: "Train number 441—Kansas City, Abilene, Pueblo, Grand Junction, and points west now ready on track 4. All abo-o-ard!"

"We're going to have to get aboard, Aunt Lorna," Roody said.

"The St. Charles's local leaves in an hour," Aunt Lorna said primly. "I'll be fine. I'll be back home by ten o'clock."

"Well—" Roody fidgeted. "Thank you for taking care of Evelyn." He pecked her maidenly cheek.

"A pleasure to have met you," Britt said ceremoniously.

She gave a lipless nod.

Roody had a firm grip on his sister's elbow. "Well, goodbye, Aunt Lorna. Give my regards to everyone. We'll have to hurry—"

They stepped off the platform, cutting across the rock ballast of the tracks. Roody clutched his sister's arm in a vise-like grip. Britt came following, beginning to feel like an unneeded tag-along. This brother-sister quarrel was none of his business.

Roody pulled out his tickets, muttering, and they went aboard the train together.

Striding impatiently through the Pullman aisle, pulling at his sister, Roody halted to glare at his tickets. "Berth 8, upper and lower. This is it." He turned aggressively. "Evelyn, I want to talk to you—"

Wriggling free of his grasp, she turned her back on her brother. "Are you in this same car, Lieutenant Pierce?" Her voice was spritely. Her ignoring of Roody was purposeful.

"No," Britt said, "I'm farther back, car 19." He eased around to pass. She restrained him.

"Won't you join us for a while?" She spoke with honey-voiced ease, as though the angry Roody had no existence.

"No." Britt knew he betrayed embarrassment, and knew he felt a growing determination to have no part in this quarrel. "I'd better get back to my berth."

"And leave me at the mercy of this beast." Her hand lay insistently on his sleeve. "It's so seldom I have an opportunity to talk to a naval officer—"

A baggage-laden porter came through the aisle, pausing: "Mr. Andrews? Miss Andrews?"

"Here," Roody said reluctantly.

"Your hand luggage, folks." He unloaded a light grip and an expensive leather portmanteau on the seat. Roody handed him a small coin.

Britt moved to follow the departing porter but the hand on his arm did not release him. Britt looked at the girl's face. It was pert and impudent and flirting, but he sensed a real urging there. It gave him the sudden impression of a child seeking to postpone punishment.

Roody said, "Oh, hell, Britt, sit down. I can argue with her later."

The porter still waited, ready to lift Britt's seabag. Britt nodded him on and handed him a dollar. He sat down.

"You're a big tipper," Roody said grumpily. He stared out the window at a moving signal lantern in the dark railroad yard.

Britt shrugged. "I travel a lot. Can't recall I've ever missed the change I've handed out tipping."

"Change? That was a silver dollar you gave that porter. Makes the rest of us look bad."

Eve said sweetly, "He's so fine, so decent—so tight."

The car was filling up with passengers, their talk an increasing undercurrent of noise. Roody sat, ignoring all but the swinging signal lamp outside the window. The train lurched suddenly in getting under way.

Eve sought to reinflame the quarrel. "What would you have had me do back there in the depot?" she said waspishly. "Let that thief steal my handbag?"

"How much money do you have in it?"

"Eighty-two cents."

Roody snorted. "And you called *me* tight!"

His sister said primly, "It's the principle."

Her brother faced her in abrupt heat. "Why can't you act like a lady? I was there. Lieutenant Pierce was there. A police officer was there in minutes. That thief wouldn't have gotten out of sight before one of us grabbed him."

"He did get out of sight," she said triumphantly.

Roody's fury burst. "I'll not discuss it!" He squirmed in an ecstasy of rage.

"What's your opinion, Lieutenant?" Her voice was sweet and baiting.

"Why"—Britt turned the cap in his hands—"I'd say you handled the situation with remarkable aplomb." He wondered at his reluctance to meet her eyes. "That is, that's what I'd say if I wasn't afraid it'd make ol' Roody here mad."

Her laughter pealed jubilantly.

Britt glanced sidelong. "They could pull the fire under the engine boiler now and use Roody."

She turned, very personally, to Britt. "Everyone calls me Eve."

Roody choked. "Stop simpering like a river-wharf tart," he gritted testily.

Britt interrupted: "Roody, it seems to me you'd appreciate the fact that your sister took care of herself so well."

"With that language? Profanity?"

The train, pulling ahead slowly, jerkily, moved out of the station.

Eve leaned to point an accusing finger in her brother's face. "I learned those cuss words from you."

The train pulled past an unlit street along which the lamplit windows of St. Louis's shantytown slums glowed yellowishly.

Britt said firmly, "I've had enough. If you two are determined to fight I'm leaving."

Roody continued to stare at the thinning lights of west St. Louis. The train pulled onto the main line and hooted a whistle blast for a grade crossing. In reflected light from the windows Britt glimpsed the crossing and the watchman standing on the grade beside the train. The watchman leaned on a cane, lackadaisically holding aloft a round wooden paddle on which was lettered STOP. A horse-drawn vehicle stood lonely in the road, awaiting the passage of the train.

The angry silence held. Britt got up to leave.

Eve said quickly, "I'm ready for a truce." She looked at Britt closely. "I don't remember you so well at that," she probed with questioning eyes.

"My father was a riverboat pilot," Britt said. "He was piloting a Union gunboat when he was killed about ten miles from your house. In the battle of Pittsburg Landing."

Roody calculated thoughtfully. "Shiloh was in '62. Seven years before you were born. But you ought to remember Britt, Evelyn."

Pierce shook his head. "No reason why she should. She was only five or six when I went to Annapolis. I only came home once or twice a year after that."

Roody said, "I haven't seen you since we moved to Kansas City."

"Roody and I used to run trotlines on Snake Creek," Britt said. "You were just a little tyke—"

"Yes," she agreed suddenly. "I remember a mudcat you and Roody came lugging in—it was bigger than I was."

"Probably," Britt said. "I was telling Roody that the last time I saw you, you were sitting on the levee blowing on a harmonica—you were about eleven."

"I probably had a pole in the river trying to catch a mudcat as big as that one you and Roody caught. I tried for years. Are you heading for Oklahoma to make the run with Roody?"

"No, I'm headed for Los Angeles. I'll make a harbor survey there, do the same in San Diego, then go to San Francisco to join our Pacific Squadron—if there's anything left to join."

"You read about the disaster off Samoa," Roody said to Eve.

"In the St. Charles paper?" she said scornfully. "That newspaper never tells about anything that happened any farther away than the St. Charles B.Y.P.U. picnic."

"B.Y.P.U.?" Britt asked.

"Button your pants up," Eve said.

"Baptist Young People's Union," Roody flared. "Evelyn, your irreverence is intolerable!"

"So was St. Charles," said Eve.

"We have family in St. Charles—" Roody appealed to Britt.

"And he's upset because he couldn't pawn me off on them all summer," Eve said.

"Our parents originally came from St. Charles. Evelyn has been there visiting just three weeks—" Roody complained.

"He meant for it to be three months," she informed Britt.

Roody leaned to confide: "She had the gall to put poor Aunt Lorna to the trouble of bringing her to St. Louis, the gall to force me to make this long trip up from Kansas City to bring her home just when—"

Eve butted in: "My little brother doesn't care how bored I get, just so he doesn't miss any fun."

"Ever since the folks were killed," Roody flared.

Britt's shock made him interrupt. "Your folks killed? When?"

"The Orpheus Theatre fire the year after we moved to Kansas City," Roody said dully. "They were attending the show that night."

Britt's glance moved from one to the other. "I believe," he said in mild accusation, "that I would be ashamed to carry on a running wrangle like this."

"I am!" Eve declared. "Roody has resented the responsibility of looking after me—"

"That's an outrageous lie," her brother charged. "*You* have resented my authority."

Britt kept trying to sidetrack the quarrel. "I remember your mother quite well," he said. "Tiny, gay, redheaded, Irish. Your father was taller. As I remember," he ventured, "they didn't get along much better than you two do."

Eve nodded. "I took after Papa. Roody looks like Mama."

"And everything that was cute on Mama is ridiculous on me," Roody groused, "the button nose, the frizzy red hair—"

Eve giggled, "I'm an inch taller than Roody."

Roody slumped against the Pullman cushions.

"I know you, little brother," Eve harried spitefully. "You look like a funny man, but you're just mean to me. You don't want me in the way."

Roody aroused to lean forward. "This is business. I should be in Arkansas City right now. I have building materials on the siding there. I'm trying to maintain a hospitality car for the trainmen—"

"And you'll be certain to get your share of the free whiskey and cigars the bank is giving them," Eve declared.

A dining-car steward sounding a musical gong passed through the aisle, announcing, "Supper is served in the dining car."

Britt asked patiently, "Do either of you ever give up?"

Roody glared at his sister. She stared back in sullen defiance.

"Let's go to the dining car," Roody suggested.

"By all means, fatty!" Eve chided. "Your chubby middle indicates your starving condition."

Roody flung himself out of the seat, nearly falling in the train's aisle. Behind him, Eve winked in mischievous gaiety at Britt. She arose with ease. Britt found himself following again, with grim doubts that supper with this pair would provide much calm.

The dining car was brightly lighted. Gleaming wall lamps glistened on white tablecloths. Polished silverware lay beside creamy china dishes. As Eve, Roody, and Britt occupied the first empty table Roody commented pompously, "Definitely an apology is due for our internecine warfare. We seem forever embroiled in a cat and dog fight."

Eve unfolded her napkin. "That's the first thing you've said that I agree with."

Roody kept on: "Our quarrels are meaningless. Brother and sister spatting. I think we both rather enjoy it."

"Speak for yourself, brother," Eve bridled. "Your idea of fun—"

Britt lifted the menu between them. "Please consider this matter of pressing interest."

It was a menu deserving consideration. A choice of clams on the half shell or *consommé printanière*. Entrées of Westphalian ham, spring lamb, or fillet of beef. For dessert sago pudding in brandy sauce, then Edam or Roquefort cheese, and French coffee.

"Dinner is table d'hôte," said Roody. "At seventy-five cents, it's more than you would expect to pay in a restaurant, but it's worth it."

They ordered while the train hurtled over clicking rails through the night. The succulent food, the warmth of the coffee, seemed to mellow even Eve's belligerence.

Roody shifted in the narrow diner chair. "I wish I could find the right bait to persuade you."

"Persuade me?" Britt finished his coffee.

"To detour south from Wichita with me and see the landrush," Roody urged. "It's going to be great, Britt. We haven't had a chance to talk in a coon's age. I can see how you might resist that but man alive, if you miss the chance to see this epic you'll blame yourself for the rest of your life."

"How about me, little brother?" Eve asked sweetly. "Who will I blame if I miss it?"

"Confound it, Evelyn, we've been over that. It's going to be a rough, frontier Donnybrook. No place for a lady."

"Since when have you considered me a lady?" Eve asked in rising heat. "Who's going to prepare your meals?"

"The last meal she cooked"—Roody lit a cigar—"she put on a pot of beans. Boiled 'em maybe twenty minutes and served 'em up as hard as rocks. Then she got mad at me when I fixed her a soft-boiled egg. She couldn't figure out how I could get it so soft, boiling it just three minutes."

Through the cloud of cigar smoke Britt reached up to pick up the dinner check and beckoned the waiter. His glance swung from Roody to Eve.

"If you'll pardon me"—Britt laid three silver dollars in the waiter's silver tray—"I think I'll skip this round."

"Keep the change," he told the waiter and left the table, leaving Roody staring moodily after him, Eve opening her lips as if in search of some new ruse to keep him at the table.

Britt moved down the center aisle, back through the train. *At least I bought their dinner*, he thought with some sense of guilt at the haste of his departure. Leaving the battling pair with the thought that they had hurt his feelings might distract them from their wrangling.

Britt found his own seat in the sleeper, then continued on to the washroom in the back of the car. As he entered the green-burlap draped washroom door he collided gently with a portly little man whose attention was fixed on buttoning his coat.

The round-faced little man looked up, declaring in a frog-like voice, "Pardon me, sir. I ought to look for oncoming traffic before I bust out through these curtains."

Britt grinned.

The little man stepped back into the washroom. When Britt had dried his hands on the roller towel, the portly man thrust out a hand.

"Judge Roland Trumbull, sir," he said in a hoarse croak. "Seeing you're a Navy man, I trust that you're not bound for Oklahoma, sir."

Britt shook hands.

"I'd surmise, conservatively," Judge Trumbull croaked, "that ninety-nine percent of these passengers are headed toward the promised land." Attention fixed on the line officer's star on Britt's sleeve, he added, "We've been reading quite a bit about you fellows, you know."

"You mean the Samoan affair?" Britt asked.

"Yes, sir. Can we talk afterwhile? Nothing secret about it, is there?"

"No," Britt replied, "just unfortunate."

"Terrible," agreed the judge. "Well, then, perhaps we can get together later for a drink in the club car." He thrust his portly waistline out of the washroom as heedlessly as before.

Britt lifted the green burlap curtain. The aisle was clear now except for a roughly dressed young man who went past—and Britt stopped short. It was the same shaggy-haired youth who had attempted to snatch Eve Andrews's purse in the St. Louis railroad station. The roughly dressed young man stepped, circumspectly, through the rear door and paused on the bounding platform between the cars.

He stood there smoking a rolled quirley cigarette held in his left hand, looking back, intently, at the spot where the portly judge had just disappeared down the Pullman aisle.

The train's roar and clicking wheels, bounding over an uneven road bed, made unremittant noise. The rough-garbed youth, apparently satisfied now that he was unwatched, flipped the quirley away with forefinger and thumb, showering sparks off into the night. He grabbed the door knob of the following car, shoved back the edge of his coarse ducking jacket and lifted a revolver from the waistband of his pants. Turning the knob, balancing himself against the rocking motion of the train, he moved to step inside the following coach.

4

Britt followed, alert and cautious. As he stepped through the rear door of the Pullman the noise of the train increased tenfold. He glanced down through the gap between the cars; the rails and ties of the road bed were a dark ribbon blurry in the night. Britt stepped across.

The entry door of the following car had a window, blackened with streaks of grime, but against the light inside the car he could indistinctly glimpse the young man's ducking jacket. The fellow was small, slightly built, wearing coarse olive drab pants and a battered felt border-campaign hat. Shaggy unshorn hair hung down over the collar of his jacket.

As Britt shoved open the car door the fellow downpointed the revolver he held and fired into the coal box beside the car's pot-bellied stove. A shower of coal chunks and dust erupted lifting into the haze of the dimly lit car.

The car was full of women. It was an emigrant car lined with wooden seats, and filled with the echoing reverberations of the gunfire. A female shriek rent the air. Women leaning forward, some half standing, their faces blanched and fear stricken, grabbed the wooden seat backs. Into this panic the young man raised the pistol and fired into the car's overhead.

Splinters flew where the bullet plowed. He reached up to seize and jerk the emergency air-brake cord. Another rending scream torn shrill and eerie from a dry throat distorted the stricken shrew face of a woman near the front of the car.

"Shut up and be quiet!" the unshorn boy shouted.

The car lurched as air brakes locked. Iron-flanged wheels

shrieked on iron rails. Britt leaped to grab the upraised pistol.

He wrapped his left arm around the youth's throat. Kneeing him, Britt lifted and threw him hard on the floor of the car wrenching away the pistol as he fell.

It was a Navy Colt, gleaming dull and oily blue in Britt's hand. The young man, flat on his back, stunned, stared up at Britt. The final jolting lurch of the train flung Britt against the wooden comfort station at the side of the car.

The youth found his wits then and scuttled back crabwise, past Britt, turning over on his belly, jerking himself up on his knees. The young outlaw seized the knob of the car door, squatting there, glaring. The train gave one last spasmodic jerk, and he stood.

In silence broken only by the hiss of escaping air from the journal boxes the young man said with grim portent, "It won't be hard to remember them brass buttons."

He jumped erect, yanking open the car door and backed retreating onto the platform between the cars. Britt pushed away from the comfort station to go after him.

The young man leaped, hurdling the guard rail, landing on the gravel ballast of the railroad track. Three men came riding out of the murky timber that lined the tracks. Two swung their horses with hard-jerked reins toward the head of the train.

The young man whistled shrilly. "It's all off," he shouted. "Pick me up, Soldier Jack!"

The third rider, a cadaverous specter, drove his horse charging up the slanting grade. The young man afoot ran toward him, half sliding, down the steep rock of the fill.

As the pair met the cadaverous rider reined his horse to its haunches in showering and cascading gravel and swung out a reaching arm. He was thin, lanky, a human scarecrow even more raggedly dressed in ill-assorted clothing than the youth he had ridden to rescue.

He yelled, "Grab a-holt, Dink!" The youth seized his arm and swung up. The doubly laden horse turned with uncertain footing down the steep fill then jumped off toward the timber.

Britt, standing on the platform, looked at the Navy Colt he still held in his hand. It was worn and old but well cared for. It had been converted to fire .38 caliber brass cartridges. It was the type weapon Britt had fired for many an hour on the Annapolis firing range.

He raised the pistol, aiming carefully at the dimming pair riding hard toward the obscure darkness of the timber. Britt eased off the trigger. The revolver flashed and roared. The youth riding behind, clinging to the cantle, howled and ducked low against the shoulder of the cadaverous man in the saddle.

Britt grinned. The bullet must have sung past that boy's ear like a wasp as he had intended. It was gratifying to know that he could still fire a Navy Colt accurately. Britt looked up toward the engine.

One of the riders there had halted, his horse milling uncertainly. The other was riding hard, straight back toward Britt. Britt pulled back the hammer, lifted the Colt, leveled it unhurriedly at arm's length, and fired again.

The oncoming rider gave inchoate shout, grabbing his right arm and clawing to keep from falling as his horse veered away toward the timber. Hasty chuffs of smoke burst from the engine's stack.

The rider who milled uncertainly near the engine cab, startled now by the frantic haste of the smoke puffs, urged his horse into motion and ran off in pursuit of his confederates toward the trees.

Britt watched this last horseman riding in awkward haste to gain the edge of the dense Missouri timber. With straining, bursting smoke puffs, engine wheels squealing and scraping to gain purchase on the rails, the train got under way.

Leaning out over the vestibule railing, Britt held the Colt at easy ready and watched the area where the outlaws had disappeared into the timber. The train gathered speed and kept pulling with hard effort. Clouds of acrid, odorous coal smoke drifted back. The snorting blasts from the engine's stack gusted in an increasingly faster pulsing beat.

Britt thumbed the revolver hammer, easing it down from full cock. He opened his coat, cached the weapon in the waistband of his pants and rebuttoned his jacket. The locomotive whistle howled in full cry as the train left the scene of the attempted holdup behind.

Lighted squares of coach windows came in sight as the train bent around a shallow curve. Britt went back inside the emigrant car.

None of the women was seated. They gathered, overwrought, in clots and groups fluctuating in size as they moved from one group to another. The din of excited female chatter rose and altered like discordant music. One lady, plump and flustered, near the front of the car clapped her fleshy hands together and called in shrill futility:

"Ladies! Ladies! I think the crisis is past. May we all be seated?"

The train's leaning angle of travel changed as it came out of the curve and bent to round a switchback. As the center of gravity shifted the women swayed like windblown reeds. The plump lady stumbled toward a wooden seat with outstretched hand and Britt reached to grasp her arm, steadying her until she recovered equilibrium.

She said flustered, "Oh!" and looked up at Britt. Recognition swept her face.

"Oh," she called loudly. All fear, doubt, and worry fled her countenance as she cried out, "Ladies, ladies! Our benefactor!"

Her cry brought the attention of a few women nearby and the clatter abated slightly. The plump lady beamed at Britt, then demanded indignantly, "What was that young man trying to do?"

"Ma'am," Britt replied gravely, "I haven't the wildest idea."

"My goodness," she said vaguely. "Oh! I'm Frances Chameau."

"Lieutenant Pierce." Britt inclined in polite salute. "Are you ladies all right?"

"I-we—" In confusion she turned to the group to call shrilly, "Ladies, are we all right?" The rising babble seemed to satisfy her. She nodded briskly, "Yes, Lieutenant, I believe we are," and she reached into a nearby group and tugged an arm.

The girl she tugged from the group could hardly have turned twenty, Britt guessed.

Mrs. Chameau said, "Lieutenant, may I present my daughter Annette."

The girl's lips were thin and pale pink in her doll-like face, but there was youthful wisdom in her eyes as she surveyed Britt. In a coolly evaluative manner she said, "How do you do, Lieutenant."

Britt directed his question to her mother. "You ladies seem to be traveling together?" And he added, "You have a lovely daughter, Mrs. Chameau."

"Youth adds strength to our cause." Mrs. Chameau's voice indicated high purpose. "Perhaps you would join us, Mr. Pierce. We would welcome a man who acts with your forthrightness and courage!"

"What cause is that?" Britt looked out over the assemblage of women.

It was a forbidding gathering. Tall, horse-faced women; short, fat women; faces grimly righteous, all with a common lack of softness, stern, unyielding, intent of eye. It made him almost anticipate Mrs. Chameau.

Her voice was ringing again. "We are a contingent of the St. Louis W.C.T.U.," she announced. "I am the chairwoman of our group." She had fully recovered her composure.

Britt commented dryly, "That is interesting."

The assortment of middle-aged and elderly women swayed with the rocking motion of the train.

The crusading ardor of Mrs. Chameau's words battled against the overriding racket of the train. "We have an opportunity of unparalleled nature. We are bound for Logan Station. There a new town will be born overnight. We are determined that new-born innocence shall prevail in that town."

Her voice rose another step: "We will be at Logan Station from the first and our presence will insure a town free from alcohol! We will defeat the demon rum before it gains a foothold. Think of it. A town free of the terrible corrupting influence of alcohol. We shall set this perfect town before the world as an example. To show others how cities large and small can achieve this perfection. Simply by outlawing whiskey and beer!"

She was interrupted by a smattering of applause from the ladies in the car.

"We would be delighted to have the assurance of your help," said Mrs. Chameau. "You and all of your fellow train workers who operate this train!"

Annette laid her hand on Mrs. Chameau's arm and said, "Mother—"

Mrs. Chameau patted her daughter's hand patiently. "Isn't there a brotherhood of trainmen—"

"Mother." A flush pinked Annette's face. Insistently she sought her mother's attention.

Britt smiled mildly, "I'm sorry, ma'am, but I'm not a member of the train crew."

Mrs. Chameau paused. "But—your uniform—"

Annette's blush deepened. "Lieutenants don't operate trains, Mother. Lieutenant Pierce's uniform is a Navy uniform!"

Annette's comment struck home. Mrs. Chameau fell victim to confused flustering. She stammered, "Oh—oh—"

"It's quite all right." Britt bowed. To Annette he said, "A pleasure to have made your acquaintance, miss."

Returning to his own car, Britt paused beside his Pullman seat long enough to remove the revolver and thrust it down among the gear in his seabag. Rebuttoning his jacket, he walked on forward through the swaying cars.

The diner was empty except for waiters at work cleaning up

the mess that had resulted from the sudden stop of the train. Midway up in the car forward of the diner, around the seats of Eve and Roody Andrews, a crowd had gathered.

Touching the luggage rack for balance Britt moved on and as he came near the group the mournfully harmonious notes of a mouth organ cut through the train noise to reach his ears.

Through the crowd of standing passengers Britt saw the cascade of Eve's springy red hair.

She was sitting atop the seatback, one high-buttoned shoe beating the rhythm on the seat, while she blew the rhythmic notes of *The Ballad of Jesse James* through her harmonica. The conductor stood beside her clicking his ticket punch.

Roody sat abjectly by the black window. The rest of the crowd was well entertained. As Britt joined them he grinned and Eve cut off her spirited playing and announced, "Here's your hero."

The conductor turned and nodded. "That's him. I told you he was wearing a Navy uniform."

"And," Eve declared, "we said pridefully we know him! He is the childhood friend of my brother!"

She looked down at Roody. "My stick-in-the-mud brother."

With her harmonica, Eve pointed at a slender young man leaning against the seat in front of her. She ordered Britt: "Shake hands with Nate Richter, Lieutenant Pierce. Nate is a gentleman of the press. He'll be wanting to interview you."

The newspaperman reached Britt's offered handshake, asking pleasantly, "Any idea who the outlaws were, Pierce?"

Britt grinned. "Like the music said, Jesse James I guess."

Sullenly, from the seat below, Roody Andrews grumbled, "Jesse James was killed in St. Joseph seven years ago."

A heavy young man in clerical collar and muttonchop whiskers leaned against the seat by Richter. He commented, "I'm guessing it was the Casey gang."

Eve said, "Our chubby friend here is Reverend Obadiah Quigley, on his way to build a church and save all the sinners who claim town lots in Logan Station. Meet Lieutenant Pierce, Reverend."

The hand Britt reached to grasp was a fist full, but friendly.

"They called the boy who jumped off the train 'Dink,'" Britt said. "Incidentally, he was the same rough who tried to take your purse in the St. Louis depot. He called the gent who picked him up 'Soldier Jack.'"

"That would be the Caseys," Richter agreed. "The other two would be Dink's brothers, Bulldog and Bung Casey."

Eve ripped off a fanfare on the mouth harp. "I should have kicked him in the groin instead of the knee." Again, she used the harmonica to point.

"Yonderly," she said, "is Peardeedo."

Sitting alone, across the Pullman aisle, was a small Mexican youth. The thin mustache hanging over the edges of his lips indicated that he was no boy, but he did not seem very old. Eve's pointing and the attention focused upon him melted what little self-confidence as he might have had. He fumbled with a frayed buttonhole in his jacket. Then almost desperately, he stood up and removed a guitar from the luggage rack overhead.

It was an instrument of rich brown wood, clearly his treasure. His slender fingers explored the strings, adjusted the tuning, and fell into a chording accompaniment. His voice, soft with Mexican accent, rose above the flowing accompaniment:

> "Oh Deenk Casey ees a fright,
> He rob with all hees might,
> With Bulldog, Bung, and Soldier Jack—
> *Pues se frustra* on thees night
> *Hombre del mar* geev heem a fright
> *Y el* train run aw-a-y down the track!"

The burst of applause that exploded from the crowd outdid the train noise.

Nate Richter said, "Great!"

The Reverend Quigley asked smilingly, "Where are you bound, Peardeedo?"

"I work to beeld thees Santa Fe tracks, long time—gandy dancer—you know. Now I go to ride—to see where they go." The slender fingers rested comfortably on the strings.

"First class, too, huh?" Nate Richter chuckled.

"What ees money? I had some . . . now I don't got none . . ."

"There were a couple words in your song that I didn't get," Richter admitted.

"The English for me—sometime she is not so good. Sometime the Spanish words come out," the little minstrel said.

Eve Andrews cut in roughly, "Well. How about another song?"

Brown fingers plucked guitar strings. A frown of hard concentration knotted Peardeedo's brow. Suspenseful moments passed. Then he sang:

> "O *el* choo, choo,
> *Sí, este* choo, choo,
> Thees night *puede caminar,*
> *El Marinero,*
> Shoot *los bandidos,*
> *Pues* we leave them behind far!"

When the applause had settled the Reverend Quigley mused, "Peardeedo. What a strange name."

"We have a word in our language," the young Mexican said. " '*Perdido*'—it means 'lost.' "

Britt, because of the angle at which she had lowered her head, could see the gentleness in Eve's eyes which the others could not. But she rapped the harmonica against her palm and her voice came forth as rough as a gunner's mate. "You know this one, Peardeedo?"

She put the harmonica to her lips and the tune of *La Paloma* floated, poignant and melancholy, out across the car.

Peardeedo's accompaniment fell at once in rhythm with Eve's melody. The crowd around them grew still.

Passengers now stood craning, listening, some lifting themselves precariously while clinging to nearby seat backs.

The concert kept on as the train swayed and chugged through the night. The passengers applauded a succession of Spanish tunes. Peardeedo with skillful virtuosity supported Eve's harmonica with rich chords, played melodic runs, and sang a few solos of his own.

Eve ran out of her Spanish repertoire with *Adios Muchachos*, then followed with a round of Stephen Foster. As Eve struck up *Camptown Races* Britt recalled his promise to visit with the frog-voiced Judge Roland Trumbull in the club car.

Reluctant to leave the music, Britt edged through the crowd to the front of the car and on through the train to the club car. It was virtually empty.

Judge Trumbull, pendulous jowled and glum, sat in an overstuffed chair nursing a whiskey and soda. He brightened visibly on sighting Britt and stood up, his squat height balanced well in the unsteady motion of the coach.

"Welcome, Lieutenant." The judge's hoarse greeting overcame the loud clicking rails which were then muffled by Britt's closing of the club-car door. "I was beginning to feel like a lonesome old man."

"There's quite an attraction back in the Pullman section," Britt grinned.

"So I hear," Judge Trumbull grumbled. "A music concert. Word drifted up. Everybody went back there."

The judge eased back into his chair, and relaxed in swaying submission to the motion of the train.

"Me, I'm tone deaf," he declared in good humor. "Can't tell one tune from another. Sit down, boy. What'll you have?"

Britt sat in the commodious chair opposite and commented that the judge's whiskey and soda looked fine.

Trumbull beckoned the club-car porter. They sipped in silence for a time before the judge initiated the matter on his mind.

"Otto von Bismarck got his comeuppance, didn't he?" he said gruffly.

"Through no credit to ourselves," Britt conceded.

The judge fixed Britt in penetrating gaze. "Hurt that bad, huh?"

"All three of our Pacific Squadron ships are on the rocks in Pago Pago harbor," Britt admitted.

"No hope to save any of them?" Trumbull asked.

Britt shrugged. "The *Nipsic* reports she believes she can float free. Maybe she can tow off the *Trenton.*"

"The Germans in just as bad shape?" Trumbull growled hopefully.

"Worse," Britt confirmed. "The *Eber* was thrown up on the beach. The *Olga* and *Adler* are swamped in the harbor."

"Hmph," grunted the judge. His questions grew more technical, examining German and U.S. foreign relations.

Britt found the discussion stimulating. Judge Trumbull was a clear-thinking man with plenty of horse sense. After nearly an hour of penetrating talk, Trumbull summed it up: "Then Germany's ambitions in the Pacific have been thwarted for the time being?"

Britt nodded. "And it appears that Congress has learned the consequences of a weak navy in an aggressive world."

"Don't depend on it," the judge disagreed. "I'm going to write a letter to our congressional delegation. This conversation we've had will enable me to make sense." He motioned for the club-car porter. "I'll order you another drink, Lieutenant."

"No, sir," Britt declined, "I believe I'll turn in. I have to change trains in Kansas City. We'll arrive there before sunup."

The judge rumbled on hoarsely, "Me, too, but I'm going to have a nightcap before I turn in."

"Good night, sir." Britt arose.

"I've enjoyed our talk." Judge Trumbull stood up.

"You make a good audience, sir," Britt offered amiably.

Trumbull received his fresh drink and raised it in salute to Britt. "That's the art of being a judge," he said.

Britt found the Pullman cars dimly lit and quiet as he went back through them. During his long conversation with the judge the berths had been made up. The passengers had retired.

Eve's and Roody's car, as Britt entered, was a long quiet aisle bordered with the closed green curtains of the berths. The concert was over. Britt experienced a pleasant glow of recollection, recalling Eve's capers and harmonica skill and the young Mexican's guitar virtuosity.

Britt moved swiftly along the carpeted aisle. Midway, a voice caught at him, insistent from the lower berth at his left. Britt halted. The voice said again, urgently, "Lieutenant!"

He leaned to part the berth's curtains and peer inside.

Eve lay there, clutching covers pulled tight to her chin, an impish deviltry dancing in her eyes.

She snickered. "I saw you coming."

Britt felt his skin prickle, his face flush hot.

She scooted over toward the window side of the train. "Lots of room in these lower berths," she commented.

Without a word Britt jerked the curtains shut and strode on down the aisle. He was near the end of the car before the laughter from her berth faded beneath the rumbling wheels.

5

The bell's strident clang awakened Britt. He sat bolt upright rapping his head sharply on the overhead above his berth and jagged streaks of light burst behind his eyelids.

Creaking, shrieking wheels as the locomotive ground slowly to a halt penetrated the Pullman, torturing his ears. Britt parted the window curtains.

It was foggy early morning, hardly light. In the circling swing of a signalman's lantern Britt read the stencil on a baggage truck quartering alongside: PROPERTY OF THE KANSAS CITY DEPOT. He began to dress with fumbling haste.

With cramped moves he rustled into pants and shirt, heaved his seabag out of the berth's luggage net, shoved his nightshirt in it, threw a square knot in the lanyard and jerked it tight.

Wearing his uniform cap over uncombed hair Britt scrambled down the ladder into the aisle and shouldered his seabag. His haste enabled him to catch the last straggle of debarking passengers. Muttering at his folly in missing the porter's call Britt made a hurried search of the milling crowd on the platform, which revealed neither Roody nor Eve.

Britt headed for the depot. Refusing a redcap's offer to relieve him of the seabag, he shouldered it, and shoved his way inside the depot.

Sheer good luck guided him to choose the right pair of doors as he plunged out onto the sidewalk in front of the depot. Tailing wisps of early morning fog made identities obscure. Britt was still blinking sleep out of his eyes, but the short man at the curb was Roody Andrews beyond doubt.

Long strides brought Britt alongside Roody to demand, "Where's Eve?"

Roody heard the question with a smug grin, his hands stuck deep in his pants pockets. The April Sunday morning was damp and chill. Britt correctly interpreted Roody's cocky, unperturbed air—the pocketed fists, the outthrust chest, the jaunty angle of Roody's hat on his frizzle of carrot hair.

"There she goes," Roody said.

Roody's nod indicated the tail lamps of a departing hack. Its rolling wheels disappeared in the fog at the far end of the depot's circular driveway. Britt dumped the seabag off his shoulder. Its bottom smacked hard on the rough brick walk.

"Damn!"

Roody stared at him blankly. "What's the matter?"

"I deserved the courtesy of a chance to say goodbye!"

Roody's scrutiny remained blank. "Didn't have any idea it would upset you."

"Damn it, Roody, a man has manners."

"So does she," Roody grumped, "bad ones. Takes up with every ragtag and bobtail. You saw her making up to that greaser Mexican kid last night. And the rest of that seedy mob."

Britt glanced toward the driveway exit, now empty in the murk of drifting fog.

Roody, in rising good cheer, said, "She'll be better off here in Kansas City. Let's go eat breakfast." He clapped Britt on the shoulder. "We've got a three-hour layover before the Wichita train makes up."

"I've got to shave," Britt said disagreeably.

"There's a barber shop in the depot," Roody said in cheery spirits. "I'll meet you in the Harvey House."

Britt emerged from the barber shop, shaved, talcumed and combed, brushing with irritation at the travel-wrinkled appearance of his uniform. He sought Roody then, and found him at a Harvey House table reading the Sunday paper.

A Harvey House waitress in ankle-length starched white

placed a cup of coffee before Roody as Britt seated himself at the table.

Britt took the menu she offered and asked, "Is there any place around here I can get my uniform pressed?"

Roody peered at him across the top of the newspaper. "On a Sunday morning? You Navy boys are the dudes, aren't you? Listen to this: 'Word is just received by a pony express messenger who came from Oklahoma that one of the United States marshals who left here Thursday killed two desperate characters he found in the walnut timber country. They defied arrest and fired on the marshal when he attempted an arrest.'"

Roody turned through the pages of the newspaper rapidly. "Britt, if you miss this show you're a bigger sucker than Barnum ever found."

Britt ordered flapjacks and ham and ate in silence while Roody read in silence—for a few minutes—then: "Listen to this. *Outlaws and Gamblers Prepared to Cause Trouble on Monday.* Deputy marshals crossed the Canadian River today and captured a party of seven who had entered the Oklahoma country. It is believed hundreds are concealed in the woods awaiting the 22nd. Thirty persons who were captured yesterday were released by the chief marshal. Their friends urged their release in such a manner that it was deemed prudent not to hold them.'"

Britt shook his head. "A one-track mind and a slipped knot on the vocal cords!"

Roody looked sharply at Britt. "That so? The landrush bores you? Maybe you'd rather hear this." He flipped a page to read: "Today is Easter Sunday and it will be observed in all churches in the usual elaborate manner. The music will be exceptionally fine. In addition to the programs for Easter Services printed yesterday other announcements have been received.

" 'Mass will be said at St. John's at 8 o'clock. At the 10:30 service the choir will sing Louis Dachauer's *Second Mass*, at the offertory, *Terra Tremuit*, by Bassini. The choir is composed of the following singers: soprano, Misses Janie Harwood, Etta

Maloney, and Georgiette Jones; alto, Misses Blanche Mc-
Donald . . .'"

Britt interrupted Roody's monotone, shoving his empty plate
forward to clatter against the salt and pepper shakers. "I've
finished my breakfast. Let's get out of here."

As they passed the newsbutcher's counter of boxed candy and
strung wires of dime novels, gaudy costumed Kewpie dolls and
Kansas City souvenirs, Britt found himself facing Mrs. Frances
Chameau. Half a step behind her Annette stood surveying the
lurid, violent covers of the hanging dime novels and penny
dreadfuls. Cool composure seemed to be this girl's long suite. She
transferred her glance of cool composure to Britt.

In her scrutiny Britt felt even more aware of the unkempt
condition of his uniform. Hesitantly, he said, "Good morning."

Mrs. Chameau seemed flustered. "Oh, good morning, Lieutenant Pierce. I wonder if this counter will have soda mint
tablets? Our journey seems to play havoc with my . . . my
digestion."

"I'm sure they will," Britt assured her. "Ladies, may I present
an old friend, Mr. Roody Andrews?"

Roody, with a wide-mouthed smile, wiggling as if he had a
tail to wag, removed his hat to expose his comedian's bald-wig
hairline. "Good morning, lovely ladies. On your way to join
the Easter parade?"

"No, I'm afraid not." Mrs. Chameau uncrumpled a wadded
handkerchief to dab nervously at her lips. "The local W.C.T.U.
ladies are taking our group to their homes for breakfast. They
should be here—"

Unable to withstand Annette's mild scrutiny, Britt muttered,
"I'd be a dapper sight in an Easter parade. Roody, are you sure
there isn't someplace I can find a presser?"

Annette offered a suggestion. "I'm sure our hostess will have
a flatiron in her home." Annette's calm tone made her suggestion seem entirely sensible. "Why don't you step in the wash-

room and remove your uniform. Have Mr. Andrews bring it out to me. I'd be glad to press it for you."

Britt's ready protest was silenced by Mrs. Chameau. "Certainly," she commanded agitatedly. "After what you did for us a small favor is the least"—she edged past Roody—"I must get my soda mint!"

In the washroom, Roody teetered on his heels then on his toes, impatiently curious. "What did you do for them?"

Britt unhooked the choker collar of his uniform, peeled off his coat and tossed it to Roody.

"They were in the car that boy bandit, what was his name—Dink Casey—picked to hoorah." Britt pulled off his pants and threw them across the jacket on Roody's arm.

Divested of his uniform, Britt bought a shoeshine. Then he remained perched in the bootblack's chair reading Roody's newspaper.

Roody strutted restlessly around the washroom and complained, "I can't fool around here for two hours with you sitting in your underwear. I'm going to hire a hack and ride over to the bank. I can let myself in the back door and check over the schedule of fund transfers. I've got to be sure they've arranged for adequate cash to reach me as soon as I get to Logan Station."

Britt glanced up absently and nodded. A customer approached the bootblack's stand and Britt surrendered the chair to him, climbing down to lean against the wall and continue reading the newspaper.

Ignoring the curious stares of men who entered and left the washroom, Britt perused with diminishing interest the pages of the Sunday paper. *Machine made ice will cool Kansas Citians this summer.*

Kansas City's baseball club had defeated Louisville on Saturday in the American Association. Baltimore had been leading Columbus eight to two when the game was rained out in the sixth inning. John L. Sullivan and Jake Kilrain were bound south to train for the championship fight.

He read intently a long landrush story which assured its readers that "the Atchison, Topeka and Santa Fe R.R. is absolutely the only railroad built into and operated through the new Oklahoma country," with information about the land office locations at Logan Station and Kingfisher.

The item had a strong railroad bias, assuring readers that "Kingfisher Stage Station is most easily reached via the Santa Fe to Logan Station, thence by stage. This is forty miles shorter than any other route . . ."

A porter entered the washroom, glanced among its occupants, and declared: "It sure ain't no problem to figure out who this belong to." He was carrying Britt's uniform, neatly pressed, and draped over his arm.

Britt donned the britches and choker jacket promptly and emerged from the washroom. Annette was nowhere in sight. With acute disappointment, Britt loitered across the depot waiting room.

He stood slapping his leg with the folded newspaper, and had spent ten minutes trying to unravel the chalk scrawled complexity of the smeared and number cluttered depot timetable blackboard when Roody came rushing through.

"Come on, let's get aboard. They're boarding the Wichita-Ark City sections now."

"They haven't been called," Britt protested.

"They will be. Come on."

Roody found his berth in the Arkansas City section near the rear of the train. Britt's reservation was in one of the Wichita ticketed Pullmans forward. Returning toward the club car at the rear of the train, passing the ladies' lounge, a feminine head jutted through the curtains to bring Britt up short.

He recognized the feminine head. Wisps of her springy red hair had fallen in disarray. Instead of belligerence there was wariness in the furtive glance she sent probing down the aisle.

It was Eve.

Britt stood still while his amusement and elation combined themselves into a desire to tease.

"Come out here!" he commanded.

Eve came out like a guilty child.

"Explain!" Britt ordered.

Belligerence began to rise in her eyes like mercury in a thermometer.

"That redheaded clown of a brother isn't going to leave me behind!" Her meekness was gone.

Britt clung to his pose of authority. "Don't use that tone on me."

Her meekness returned instantly, so surprising that Britt lost command, saying lamely, "I thought Roody said you had no money."

"I had an heirloom watch my grandmother gave me," she confided. "I had the hacky take me to the pawnshop."

"You found a pawnshop open on Sunday morning?"

His disbelief again raised Eve's ire. "Uncle Barney lives upstairs over his store. He and Daddy were poker-playing buddies when we first came to Kansas City. He'd open his store while Gabriel was blowing his horn if I asked him to. He wanted to *give* me the money, but I wouldn't have it. I pawned my watch!"

She had lifted herself to tiptoe, virtually prancing with inexplicable anger. Britt's emotions finally settled on amusement.

"So what are you going to do?" He grinned. "Spend the whole trip hiding from Roody in the ladies' lounge?"

She stopped prancing and her anger disappeared as inexplicably as it had arisen. She took a doubtful breath and concentrated her gaze on the carpeted aisle.

Britt took her arm. "Come on."

She held back, dragging her slight weight against his pull.

"Confound it," Britt said. "You can't live in that lounge."

Reluctantly she accepted his escort. The train suffered its first hard jolt of getting under way, emitted a groan of almost human agony at the breaking of its inertia-locked joints, and was beginning to roll as they entered Roody's car.

Roody was looking out of the window beside his seat, mildly entranced by the panorama of waving hands and arms, raised hats, fluttering handkerchiefs and blown kisses being thrown toward departing passengers from the passing platform outside the Pullman window.

Britt said, "Roody—"

Roody's pug-nosed glance lifted expectantly. Then his face went choleric. "Unholy hell's fire and damnation!"

6

After a late morning stop at Topeka the train chuffed into the afternoon, puffing its way down through the flint hills of Kansas.

Roody's first fury at discovering his sister aboard the train had left him incoherent. He had fumed and stuttered, finally recovering to accuse Britt.

"You let her wheedle you into conspiring—she found you and you—"

"No, I found her," Britt contradicted.

"—you bought her ticket," Roody wrathfully accused and when Britt had denied this Roody stormed off, weaving down the aisle of the unsteady train, rebounding off the seat backs he passed.

Britt and Eve still sat together in the seat Roody had vacated. The Pullman was crowded. Settled into the irregular rhythm of motion, above the regular click of the rails, the steady roar of wheels on rails, the dulling incessance of many voices, blurred in indistinguishable words, the hours lagged by in travel wearying dullness.

Britt and Eve's conversation lapsed into spells of long silence, far spaced statements and responses, yet the thread of it was not lost. They drowsed, half asleep, as the vastness of the flint hills and Kansas grasslands unrolled outside the train window.

Across the landscape the roll of dark jutting rocky draws and low hills spread to dimly perceived horizons. There were few trees, and scatterings of cattle. A faint pastel brownish green tinted the vast rolling landscape. Spring grass was coming, a sight Britt found lifting his spirit with its freshness.

The sun sent lancing shafts of light through the broken clouds adding to the vasty aspects of this enormous country, and burning away the drab veils of fog that had cloaked the day past noon.

Cotton white clouds towered, bunched, and drifted across the sky, softening the aspect of these rugged Kansas hills. It was a huge, lost land, devoid of human habitation.

"There is not only the danger," Britt commented to Eve thoughtfully, urgently, "there are the plain facts of hardship, and of disorganization."

From the floor where it had fallen, he retrieved the Kansas City *Morning Globe* and opened it to the front page. "This rough and tumble landrush you're determined to jump in the middle of is surely no place for a woman. TWO TEAMSTERS DROWNED WHILE FORDING SWOLLEN STREAM" he quoted a headline, and read aloud the *Globe* correspondent's report of a Kansas contingent of landrush boomers crossing the Salt Fork River in Indian Territory. They had torn up a depot platform in the Ponca Indian nation and used the lumber to make a temporary wagon bridge out of a railroad bridge.

"*Two foolish teamsters who would not await their turn rushed into the river and attempted to ford it,*" Britt read. "*They were swept away and lost before our eyes. We were powerless to save them. A cry of horror went up from thousands of throats at the terrible sight. The next bad spot we will encounter will be Bear Creek crossing, but all hope for the best.*"

"So do I," Eve said. "I'm curious." She pointed at the column covering the Navy's troubles in Samoa. "Why don't you ever talk about that?"

Britt folded the paper. "You've never asked me to."

"I just did."

Britt watched the passing landscape with a half-seeing stare. "Very well. The Navy has been neglected by Congress ever since the Civil War. Rotting, poorly manned ships. A corrupt Navy Secretary in the President's cabinet in Washington. You understand I could be court-martialed for what I'm saying—"

"My lips are sealed," Eve said virtuously.

"Ships built of green timber, falling apart, hardly able to leave the Navy yard before needing repairs. Other nations building iron ships, converting to steam, our ships mongrel fusions of wood and iron. Steam propulsion jammed into wooden hulls still carrying masts and sail. Hodgepodge ships like the *Nipsic*, *Vandalia*, and *Trenton* ordered to Samoa to confront formidable new beauties like Germany's *Adler*, *Olga*, and *Eber*—"

"Why?"

"Otto von Bismarck is ambitious," Britt said. "He wants Samoa for a coaling station for his new iron ships. A bully has to be confronted where he challenges."

"How do you think it will end?" Eve asked.

"It already has ended. In disaster for both sides," Britt said. "While our fleet and the Germans sat glaring at each other over their guns a typhoon swept the harbor. Every vessel wrecked. By Yankee luck we are the winner by virtue of the fact that von Bismarck is out of business for a while, and our Congress has been jarred into action. Which is the reason for my orders. I'll report in Los Angeles, then continue to San Francisco. Our yard and dock facilities must be expanded. Then I'm due for a tour of sea duty in the Pacific."

"How exciting." She sounded carelessly cynical. "You're on the way to the Pacific and I'm on my way to the wild western frontier to take care of myself."

Eve's attention seemed caught by the awesome sweep of prairie landscape flowing by the train window and Britt's glance followed hers, wondering how much of what he had said she had really heard. The sun-littered panorama of rock ledge-studded grassland seemed overpowering competition for his pedantic discussion of naval problems.

He studied her as she sat watching the passing scenery, oblivious to his scrutiny. She wasn't pretty. Spirited, pixie-like, impish, but not beautiful. She looked a little tired in the flood of sun-bright glare illuminating the dusky train car interior.

He could not recall ever encountering a more headstrong or frustrating person. He ceased his staring scrutiny of Eve, and looked out across the vast spreading swell and draw of the land. The prairie was marked with timber lined ravines that varied in curving, gently circling patterns. High, drifting, wind-swept cloud masses laid dark shadows on the land.

Vague forebodings troubled Britt's contemplation. Restlessly he shifted his attention to bring her profile into sharp focus. She sat quiescent, confident, the shape of hairline and brow back-lighted by the sun and bright window, her face held high.

Beyond the window the deep ravines carved their way into the hard sodded limestone prairie, losing themselves in hidden draws, obscured by blackjacks along the dry washes. Oak, walnut, the towering green cedars revealed their spring-fed sources of water. From an occasional draw a rivulet of water might wander, running out into sunlight over its bed of pebbles. Thin, clear, sparkling in the sun, presently sinking in its own bed of worn stone, to disappear beneath the grassy cover of prairie.

Britt felt a strong desire to argue with Eve. She seemed so stiff-necked and stubborn. He wished he knew her well enough to say what was on his mind, and he silently rehearsed what he ought to say. *You proud little idiot,* he thought. *Don't you realize that being inside this long iron snake wandering across this land is one thing. Outside it is another.*

We ride along in this moving island of civilization—in here are people and friendly help. If you get sick, if you are injured, someone will take care of you. But outside the iron-skinned refuge of this train lies a land that is as beautiful as it is terrible.

Out there in that lovely, soft-grassed land is careless death. If you fall out there, there is no one. If you are injured you can suffer and die alone.

It is a lovely, deceptive trap. Those branches, leafy and green, hide thorns that tear civilized clothes. Along those clear streams the cotton-mouth water moccasin glides. In those glistening limestone ledges the diamond back rattlesnake lives.

The timber wolf has powerful jaws that can rend your flesh. Those birds that glide in high soaring grace through the warm updrafts are buzzards, seeking the flesh of the dead to devour. The prairie is like the sea, beautiful in ratio to its utter deadliness.

In this merciless environment, empty, devoid of human help, you'll "take care of yourself?" As he thought he found himself growing more angry until, in his imagination, he was almost shouting at her, *Hellsfire girl, it is like this for a thousand miles to the south, beyond the Texas border and into Mexico. A country of nothingness, where a hardened man can meet with a small misfortune, and die alone.*

But he suppressed his desire and rode in silence. Britt guessed that neither reasoning nor profane raging was likely to prevail on her headstrong determination. She had heard the raging and shouting, from Roody. She would interpret Britt's concern as she had interpreted Roody's yelling efforts to influence her—just an attempt to get her out of the way so the men could enjoy all the excitement and have all the pleasure.

So Britt withheld, and controlled his temper. He remembered Eve's purposeful cussing in the St. Louis depot. *There's no use,* he thought. *I'll not let myself in for a tirade from her sharp tongue.* He pondered in silence, seeking another way, and found none.

He made his way aft through the restless aisle traffic, through three crowded Pullmans to the club car. He wondered if the emigrant car with its dedicated female W.C.T.U. cargo was somewhere in the train, perhaps forward among the day coaches? *Maybe all the women in the world are going crazy,* Britt thought.

The club car was full. In a corner red mohair lounge, surrounding a small table covered with loaded ashtrays, scattered playing cards, and iced glasses, sat four people.

Roody was one of them. Britt edged across. Roody stood up

with unstable, careful politeness as Britt approached. Britt examined his carrot-topped friend's eyes. They were unfocused, slightly glazed.

Roody called out heartily, "Britt! Join us!" and he addressed his companions, "Let me present Lieutenant Britt Pierce, U.S.N."

Roody leaned and steadied himself with a splayed short-fingered hand against the wall of the train. He made a sweeping gesture toward the couple seated beside him.

"Mr. and Mrs. George Basil, Britt."

Roody then pointed a stubby finger at a beefy two-hundred and fifty pounds of tough Chicago tenderloin gambler. "This is Mister Horst Stutz," Roody slurred.

Without arising, Mister Horst Stutz offered his huge hand. He was waistcoated, gold-toothed, ruby-studded, and prosperous. Britt had seen his breed in waterfront saloons around the world.

The other man appeared disarmingly commonplace. Britt passed over the iron gray ordinariness of George Basil's suit, the paleness of his cravat, observed the hard-lined thinness of his face, and his eyes.

The pale steel gray of Basil's eyes suggested to Britt that commonplace outer appearance cloaked a steel-jacketed will, and a multi-horsepower brain. The woman beside him was lush.

Britt repelled a strong impulse to whistle. He said, "Roody, I'd like to talk to you for a minute."

Roody worked his way out of the red upholstered corner to make unsure progress among adjoining tables out of the car. As they stood together in the noisy privacy of the train's rear observation platform, Britt decided Roody had had too much to drink. Experience with drunks, as a junior officer in charge of boating liberty parties back to the ship from foreign beaches, had taught Britt not to expect much success in a situation like this.

Roody, with bleary shout, declared, "I cannot understand why such a charming woman would marry a man like George Basil."

The train noise here was overpowering.

"Known them long?" Britt yelled.

"Just met," Roody answered.

Raising his voice as if commanding a quarterdeck in the wind, Britt suggested, "Damned strange company to find a banker in."

"How's that?" Roody's query blurred.

"That's a bunch of professional gamblers," Britt said.

Roody leaned precariously against the bulkhead of the club car. "All life is chance," he declaimed expansively. "That's why I'm bound for Logan Station. I can buck the game there, take my chances and win success in a few months that would take forever in Kansas City."

Britt said flatly, "Roody, I'm worrying about Eve."

Roody's Irish face screwed up tight and anger appeared in his eyes. His red face began to turn purple, creeping down from the hairline.

"The hell with her!" he shouted. "I've got a bank to open. She wasn't asked to come!"

Britt turned and left Roody standing on the platform. In the sound of chatter as he re-entered the club car the memory of Roody's shouted *the hell with her* re-echoed in his senses.

The door of the club car banged shut behind him, then opened again as Roody entered to rejoin his friends. Britt paused and heard the whiskey thick accent of Roody's voice, in burlesque Irish dialect, cry out at the bejeweled Mrs. Basil, "Inez, me bitter sweet beauty—"

Britt thought *the hell with that* and moved on. Proceeding up through the long succession of crowded aisles, he sought the conductor, and found him in the dining car's narrow kitchen. The conductor was leaning against the serving counter, drinking coffee with the steward.

Britt handed him his ticket, "I wonder if I could change cars?"

The conductor squared his hat as if to assume an official demeanor and looked at the ticket. "What's the matter?"

"I'm in the Wichita section," Britt said.

The conductor handed the thick white cup and saucer to the

steward, fingered the strip of Pullman ticket and said gruffly, "I can see that."

"I'd like to change to the Arkansas City section."

"We'll switch that section off in the Wichita yards along about dark. You're bound for Los Angeles."

"I *was* bound for Los Angeles," Britt affirmed.

"Well, you can't get there on the Ark City section," the conductor argued. "The Wichita section highballs on west through New Mexico, to California."

Britt said, "I want to change where I'm going. I want to go to Arkansas City."

The conductor looked Britt up and down, carefully, his gaze lingering. "Are you the fellow that prevented the holdup on the westbound flyer out of St. Louis?"

Britt admitted, "I guess I am," and felt a vague embarrassment.

There was no humor in the conductor's level stare. "The Missouri-Pacific conductor said you were seafaring—a Navy fellow. Said he thought you were boarding my train. Train holdups are no joke."

Britt reached inside his jacket for his wallet.

"Landrush bug bit you?" asked the conductor.

Britt shook his head.

The conductor speculated. "I never heard of a lieutenant going over the hill."

Britt made a small grin. "I've got a little time." He opened his wallet, and it was the conductor's turn to lack humor. "I'm no headwaiter. You can't bribe me."

Britt smiled. "I'd like to purchase a ticket from Arkansas City on south to—I think you call it Logan Station. I just intend to pay my fare."

"That Ark City section is already crowded."

Britt shrugged without argument.

"It's the Missouri-Pacific owes you a favor, not the Santa

Fe." The conductor's face began to lose its grimness in a reluctant smile.

Britt offered no persuasion, but he waited.

"I'm not expecting any holdups"—the conductor's grin widened—"but you'll keep your eyes open, won't you?" He figured the amount on the margin of Britt's ticket, accepted the money, and wrote a lengthy notation on the portion of the ticket he handed back to Britt. "I'm an habitual sourball, Lieutenant. It's a pleasure to have you on my train. Every trainman appreciates what you did. We never know when it's our turn next."

"Thank you," Britt said.

"I'll try to find somebody in the Ark City section who's getting off at Wichita to swap berths with you. Wouldn't want you to have to sleep standing up."

Britt returned to the Pullman. Eve was missing from the seat where he had left her. He worked his way back through the crowded train. In the club car, Roody sat alone. Seeing Britt, Roody waved an invitation.

Britt shook his head and proceeded on to the rear platform of the train. No Eve.

Re-entering, he saw Roody making his way unsteadily down the aisle. Britt let Roody fight his way in precarious instability through the swinging, banging doors of the between cars vestibules. Roody finally made it, to sink dizzily into his seat in his own Pullman.

Eve entered the opposite end of the car, almost dancing down the aisle in short steps to keep her balance on the heaving aisle floor.

"I was looking for you," she informed Britt.

Britt said neutrally, "I just came through this whole train."

Her eyes sparkled mischievously. "Then there must be a few nooks you can't enter."

The tall newspaperman Richter came loping down the aisle. "I thought I saw you headed this way," he told Eve.

The three stood together in the aisle.

Eve asked the journalist, "All set for the land race?"

Richter nodded assent. "I'll go down on the press car. I've got a flatbed press and a few fonts of type standing somewhere on the freight dock at Logan Station. Hope to be printing the news by Tuesday."

The sound of a long, guzzling snore floated up. Britt turned to look. Roody was stretched out and dozing, occupying the whole seat.

"Let's go back to the club car," Eve suggested, "so we won't disturb the sleeping beauty."

As they passed through the vestibule the young Reverend Quigley met them, balancing a large cardboard carton held in both hands. Eve caught the Reverend's arm and they gathered inside the entry of the club car.

Brashly direct, Eve queried, "What's in the box, preacher?"

"The good ladies of the church in Kansas City packed me a generous supper and sent me on my way rejoicing."

The car door slammed open. As if blown in on a gust of wind the slight, brown-faced man, guitar slung across his back was swept into the car. Peardeedo stopped before Eve.

"I think that I seen you—"

"—coming this way," Richter and Quigley spoke in unison.

"We have a Greek chorus," Eve grinned wryly.

"And food for the entire cast," Quigley offered. "Won't you join me? The good ladies far overestimated the capacity of even a Methodist minister."

Britt accepted a piece of fried chicken and a bread-and-butter sandwich. Deviled eggs passed from hand to hand. As they settled down to eating, the Reverend announced, "Mrs. Quigley will be coming to Logan Station to join me after the Run, as soon as the confusion is over."

"You're married?" Eve's dismay was dramatically magnified. "That does it for you! I thought you were an eligible bachelor."

"Have another piece of chicken," Quigley suggested.

The conversation went on. Britt, naturally reticent and accustomed to the formal social restraints of military life, marveled at how quickly these four fell into an easy, relaxed relationship.

Peardeedo emerged from his shell of self-effacement to announce that he had been offered a job at Logan Station.

"How?" Eve demanded. "You haven't even been there yet."

"There are two men," Peardeedo explained, "*los Señores* Stutz and Basil. They go to open a place of entertainment there. I am hired to play, to sing *canciones* in their place of entertainment."

Richter asked in reportorial curiosity, "How do they know you'll be any good?"

"*Anoche*—the last night—" he slid the guitar from his back and fingered an arpeggio, adulation toward Eve mirrored in his eyes—"when we play and sing in the coach, they are near. They hear."

"More chicken, Peardeedo," offered Reverend Quigley.

"No, *padre. Estoy harto, lleno hasta aquí*," Peardeedo lifted a hand to his throat to indicate how full he was.

There are no strangers out here, Britt thought. A meeting meant immediate intimacy, as if they had been acquainted for years instead of being thrown together by chance for a night's travel on the train.

"Señorita," Peardeedo suggested timidly, "those men. They hear you, too. They like to hire you *tambien*."

"I'll keep it in mind," Eve said wryly. "I'm going to be short of money."

"A female vagrant," Richter grinned wryly. "I'll keep an eye on you." He turned to the preacher. "Maybe I can expose some scandal for you to combat."

"A lofty motive." The young preacher laid aside a chicken bone and mopped his fingers with his handkerchief.

"Those men. They like you, *mucho*." Peardeedo's eyes rolled, "ay, ay-yi!"

"Peardeedo"—Eve leaned to kiss the Mexican's cheek—"that's for getting the job offer for me."

"Lascivious, too!" Richter grinned wolfishly. "You're scandal bait—and scandal sells newspapers!"

"There is a broad difference," Reverend Quigley said piously, "between an honest expression from a warm heart and loose conduct."

But Quigley's gaze was fixed on Eve with a quizzical eye, it seemed to Britt. It occurred to Britt that the preacher's soft appearance was a puzzle. Britt sensed a tough fiber in Obadiah Quigley. Once on a course Quigley might be battered by the winds of opposition, but he might obtain his objective through unremitting obstinacy.

Nate Richter warned, "Don't get ringy, preacher. I'm cynical enough to recognize a loose woman when I see one."

"Do you see one?" Eve asked thinly.

Richter met her suddenly angry stare unevasively.

"No, ma'am!" he said.

She relaxed.

Richter had the untanned face of indoor work. Pallid in the artificial illumination of the club car, even in a kidding mood, zeal still smoldered in his eyes.

Britt said mildly, "Eve, you just won an encounter with the editor and I suspect he doesn't lose many arguments."

"She overawed me," Richter said with stoic candor.

The preacher was repacking lunch papers and trash in his carton. He shoved it beneath the seat.

"Any jackass who implies I'm a loose woman had better get ready to lose an encounter." Eve turned cold eyes on Britt.

"And take the risk of acquiring marks of tooth and nail, I suspect," Obadiah Quigley added with solemn nod.

Peardeedo's fingers plucked modulating chords from the guitar. They became an accompaniment. Eve nodded. She picked up the melody. Her voice, high and sweet, in silver clarity, sang the words:

"In the gloaming . . . oh my darling . . . When the lights are soft and low . . ."

Silence fell through the crowded car. Eve's song carried above the click of passing rails and the crowd seemed subdued by it. Tone glistening, of fragile, angelic beauty, and Britt wondered.

Which was real? The Eve of curse and kick? The temptress who devilishly invited him into her Pullman berth? Whose mischief could turn to vicious anger and goad her brother into fury? She could destroy anyone's composure. Now she was a friendly girl of open countenance who won everyone's friendship. Richter and Quigley were men of mind and spirit, and they had been won by her. She obviously held the full adoration of the little Mexican guitarist.

Eve had made Peardeedo the center attraction of this gathering in which he might otherwise have been the butt of jokes. Her singing silenced a trainload of rough frontiersmen bound hellbent for a western landrush.

Her song had simply melted them into quiet. Britt scanned the jammed club car. It was filled with male faces. Some of them were hard faces.

Eve's song, the progressions of Peardeedo's guitar seemed to engender a warmth of days gone, of friends and family, all resolved in harmony. Long after the song, the silence held. A silence underlaid by clicking rails and the flow of night passing outside the train window.

And in the quiet Britt Pierce wondered.

7

The party enlivened.

Eve's high spirits infused other passengers. Men offered songs. Witticism flew across the club car—some of it ribald. Britt watched the sensitive young preacher wince, shocked by each shouted vulgarity. It did not seem to disturb Eve.

She was buoyant, and crowded open a space in the center aisle when Peardeedo came tugging the porter from the club bar. Whistling his own syncopated jazzband tune through his teeth the porter performed a buck-and-wing.

Britt saw a whiskey bottle being passed. Men hunkered in the aisle, stood on seats, sat on seat backs. The bottle was soon out of sight. The porter executed his tricky steps in the unstable aisle as agilely as if he were on a vaudeville stage. As he finished in arm-waving climax Britt slipped a silver dollar into the porter's palm.

Someone in the crowd caught the gesture, which precipitated a hail of silver from all over the car. Into the confusion the conductor stepped, dodging flying coins.

"Ed," he complained to the porter, "isn't what you win off me at pinochle enough?"

The porter winked. "I can afford to *lose* a little now."

The conductor spoke to Britt, "Here's your new Pullman berth number, Lieutenant."

"I'd like to thank the man who traded," Britt offered.

"No call to. It was an equal swap."

"Then I'll thank you."

"You already have," the conductor replied and smiled. "Watch out for those holdups."

He moved on through the car, lifting his hat to Eve. Britt watched her trying to make her way back from the far side of the crowd that had watched the buck-and-wing. She seemed completely at ease with men. Britt could see her lips move as she exchanged wisecracks with the men she squeezed past and Britt felt a sparse admiration at her ability to mingle.

The edge of Britt's glance caught the Reverend Obadiah Quigley observing her, his face quizzical.

Britt wedged through the press of men and asked, "What do you think, parson?"

With raised eyebrows, cocking his head, "Of Eve Andrews?" Quigley pondered. "The Methodist discipline, I fear, would render harsh judgment of her—and of me for participating in such levity." His cherubic face turned guileless. "Speaking personally, Lieutenant, I'm having a fine time, and in my judgment Miss Andrews has a remarkable gift."

Eve arrived to exclaim, "Goody! Give it to me!"

"What?" Quigley asked.

"My gift!"

"Rather," said the preacher, "I wish you could give some of it to me."

Eve pinched his cheek.

Britt said to her, "If you can descend for a moment I'd like to say good night."

A sobering touched her eyes. Perhaps it was bitterness. She said, "You mean goodbye."

She added, "Before morning we'll be through Wichita."

"Through Wichita we'll be," he agreed.

She paused. "I'll be in Arkansas City. You'll be on your way to the Coast. Don't you want to come tuck me in?" The same inviting coquetry he had seen once before in her eyes sparked challenge.

Britt glanced at Nate Richter, at Peardeedo, at the preacher, at the crowding men of whom she was the center of attention. "I think you'll be able to recruit a volunteer to tuck you in," Britt said. "Good night."

He was surprised at the bitterness in his own voice.

She said, "Goodbye, Lieutenant," and turned away.

Britt was unable to tell whether she sounded wistful, or angry, or cynical.

He stood pensively, watching her leave, wondering why he had not told her he would be on the train with her to Arkansas City, to Logan Station, and Nate Richter's question jarred rudely into Britt's confused self-probing.

Richter asked, "Heard anything from the Casey gang?"

Britt had trouble refocusing his thoughts . . . the Casey gang . . . his attention came around with reluctant slowness. From vague recollection he replied a vacant, "No."

"You will," Richter declared, his reedy voice insistent.

Britt made no reply.

"That bunch is well wanted," Richter went on laconically. "They couldn't be guilty of all they're accused of. But there is enough. They were all recognized in spite of disguises when they held up a South Dakota bank last Christmas. Soldier Jack had disguised himself as Santa Claus."

Britt smiled wryly. "A timely disguise."

"One thing the Caseys didn't anticipate. A bunch of kids followed Santa Claus into the bank. The Caseys killed two of those youngsters when they got nervous and started shooting wild inside the bank."

Britt's beginning smile turned cold and sickly. "And the gang got away." Richter had his attention in focus now. "The Caseys grabbed kids for hostages." Richter nodded. "The townspeople were afraid to shoot back for fear they'd hit their own children. One four-year-old boy got his leg broke when Bulldog Casey threw him away as their horses ran out of town."

Britt's imagination conjured up the scene well enough.

"They're an unholy lot," Richter said grimly. "I think they've been hiding out down in Indian Territory between depreda-tions. They probably know that Oklahoma country better than the Army. We had a wire report on a store holdup over by Muskogee couple months ago. Storekeeper didn't have any money so one of the outlaws beat him to death, then they all raped his wife. Four men, and the wife's description of the brute who beat her husband to death sounds like Bung Casey."

The thoughts passing through Britt's mind reminded him that Dink Casey would clearly remember Eve for thwarting him in the St. Louis depot. He remembered the young outlaw's threat that he would remember the brass buttons on Britt's own uni-form after the attempted train robbery.

He heard Richter ask, "Have you got a gun?"

"I've got Dink's gun," Britt reminded Richter.

"Do you know how to use it?"

Britt looked at Richter in surprise. "It's a Navy Colt."

Richter's sardonic smile admitted the naiveté of his question. "I guess I wouldn't ask a fish if it knew how to swim," he admitted.

"You think the Caseys will turn up in Logan Station?" Britt guessed.

Richter nodded. "I think they'll turn up in Arkansas City. Anywhere there's a crowd, and money, with people preoccupied like this landrush crowd. The Casey boys like to turn up and relieve people of their money while they're preoccupied."

Britt suddenly and inexplicably felt very tired. He looked around. The crowd in the club car had thinned perceptively. The preacher was gone. Peardeedo was nowhere in sight. Nate Richter, having delivered himself of dire warning, was fashion-ing a rice-paper cigarette, apparently satisfied with the disturb-ing worry he had added to Britt's already potent concern over Eve.

Richter hung the cigarette on his lip and began prowling his pockets for a match. Britt left the club car, walking forward through the train to the Ark City Pullman section. Roody, still snoozing against the dark brown mohair seat, was sprawled there, his mouth agape, emitting the guzzling sounds of deep slumber.

The silence, the lack of motion, gradually fetched Britt from sleep. After days of jarring, muscle-wearing train vibration, the lack of motion startled him momentarily, and then he relaxed in it, utterly comfortable. He lay slack, breathed deeply, turned over and sat up.

Cautiously, avoiding the low overhead, Britt dressed. As he came down the ladder out of his upper berth, Eve, legs first, emerged from her lower berth not far forward in the car.

When she was erect, Britt said, "Good morning."

Eve's head rotated, her disbelief apparent. Then her entire demeanor changed, as if merriment rose effervescent in her.

Her joy communicated itself to Britt.

He grinned. "I decided Roody is right. I can't afford to miss that landrush."

With both hands Eve took his arm. "Take me to breakfast!" she ordered.

To Britt, even her order seemed happily remarkable, as though they experienced an equality of delight. They proceeded through the Pullman aisle, into the vestibule, and Britt handed her down the iron steps to cindered ballast.

The Pullman was one in a string of cars, standing without engine or tender, parallel to other strings of coaches lining every siding in Arkansas City's railroad yards.

Eve squeezed his arm. "I'm glad you decided to stay."

In this state of euphoria Britt touched her hand on his arm. "I've calculated my time. I can catch a train out of your Logan Station on Wednesday and arrive in Los Angeles without being overleave."

From an emigrant coach ahead ladies began to descend. At their head, Britt saw Mrs. Chameau. It was the W.C.T.U. delegation. As Britt and Eve approached, the stern and tired-appearing ladies came pair by pair from their boxcar-like coach.

Annette Chameau came last from the car. Lagging behind, she caught up her skirts to hurry.

Britt called, "Wait a moment!"

She turned. Weariness marked but did not mar her smooth-cheeked young beauty. As always she seemed fully composed, seeming almost to send forth waves of tranquillity.

Britt said, "Miss Andrews, may I present Miss Chameau?"

Both girls looked at Britt, as if expecting something further. He said nothing and both girls looked away with murmured polite phrases.

Annette was saying, "I had better hurry," and turning to glance at the distance she had fallen behind she ran away.

Britt and Eve walked on. Abruptly Eve released his arm.

Her words were clipped and short as she said, "The party broke up too early last night. That gang thins out fast. I went to bed but I couldn't go to sleep." Again her demeanor had completely changed. She seemed angry.

Perplexed, Britt lost the context of what she was saying. Her rapid chatter jarred his nerves. He wondered what had happened to the pleasant rapport they had been sharing. She ceased her chatter abruptly and they walked along in silence.

Reaching the end of the long string of cars, Arkansas City's business street came in view. The procession of W.C.T.U. ladies was marching along, making way through pedestrian traffic like a ship cleaving a wake.

The pedestrians they met, almost all males, moved aside with doffed hats, then stared after the female procession. Some men looked curiously down the street as though expecting something to follow, perhaps flag bearers, or a burst of martial music.

After the parade of militant females had passed men drifted together in groups. As Britt and Eve approached one of the groups Britt heard chuckling laughter in response to some salty remark made by one of the men.

Eve said, "I thought all W.C.T. ewes were old and ugly."

Britt missed the pun.

The W.C.T.U. procession turned down a side street.

"*Quo vadis?*" Eve asked.

"I expect they're bound for breakfast. In Kansas City some church ladies fed them."

"I was sure you'd know," Eve said. "Those kill-joys take care of each other. They have chapters everywhere."

"Where they're headed there'll be no chapter to take care of them," Britt mused.

"God will provide."

"Let's find some breakfast," Britt suggested mildly.

"This town has nothing but greasy spoon cafes," Eve complained.

In the one they tried the busy counter girl apologized. "These boomers swarm like locusts. All we have left is oatmeal and coffee."

After they had eaten and returned to the sidewalk Britt stood brushing his uniform.

"What you need," Eve proposed, "is butternut britches and a pair of boots."

She pointed over the tops of passing vehicles to the BOSTON STORE: Outfitters and Clothiers. "Let's try over there." They crossed dusty ruts and horse droppings steaming in the chill morning air. Britt completed his purchases quickly, and was removing his uniform in a curtained dressing cubicle when he heard Eve ask the middle-aged clerk brusquely, "Do you have the same things in my size?"

The clerk's reply was hesitant with embarrassment. "For a lady—men's pants? I suppose we have nearly the same, in boys' sizes."

Britt folded a pants leg to lace inside his high leather boots. *She is as unpredictable as rain in a dry country,* he thought, then it occurred to him, *think what is least likely and she'll sure do it.* The thought that followed, *she'll be coming in here to change in a minute*, struck him and he began to hurry frantically.

He heaved a sigh of relief when he heard the embarrassed clerk point out the store's other dressing room to her.

When Britt came out, Eve was already seated in the shoe department, wearing the pants and shirt, pulling a pair of thick, muckled brown cotton socks on her bare feet.

The clerk's face, red as a fireman's shirt, was beginning to streak with sweat.

"I—I'm afraid I've never," he stammered, "I've never fitted a lady's foot with a boot before."

"Feet are feet," Eve said impatiently, "whatever they're fixed on. Quit squirming and let me see what you've got."

"I—I'm—only a boy's size—" He arose to fumble through a stack of boxes, secured one, dropped it and scrambled to retrieve the footgear, packing tissue, and box.

Eve took the boot, held it at arm's length, and exclaimed, "Copper toes? Look, Britt! They've even got a jackknife here in this little pocket. Isn't that handsome?"

Her dexterous fingers, unhampered by embarrassment, facilitated the lacing and in a moment she was up stamping around the store aisle, her pants laced inside the red-leather trimmed, copper-toed boots. The clerk, with lowered head, was wrapping Britt's uniform in brown paper.

Eve snatched up her dress and underclothing from the shoe-department seat where she had left them and carried the garments to the clerk.

"Here, wrap my stuff in the same package. You don't mind, do you?" she asked Britt.

"Why should I?" Britt shrugged in reckless abandon. "But relieve me of that stuff before I ship on out to the Coast. I'd hate to think of unwrapping that package in the *Nipsic's* wardroom!"

Eve paid her bill. As they walked back toward the depot she said, "Well, that broke me. I'm a charity case now."

She stopped short beside the tracks. "I wonder—"

Her questioning frown was fixed on a caboose that stood alone, on a spur of rusty siding dead-ended against a bunker. A trainman came out. Another entered.

"Let's go see," Eve seized Britt's elbow. An engineer in striped overalls and cap climbed the iron steps to enter the caboose.

Awkward in her new boots Eve stumbled. Ascending the black iron steps, hearing the hullabaloo inside the caboose, Britt purposefully stepped ahead of Eve and into the caboose. It was filled with men, smoke, and barroom smells.

Roody, florid and hearty, stood just inside the door passing out cigars to those who entered. He offered a cigar to Britt while still talking to the engineer who had just entered.

A bartender drawing steins of beer from a tapped keg behind the improvised bar lined steins of foaming dark brew on pine planks to await any hand that reached. Roody aimed the engineer toward the beer, and turned to Britt.

His first greeting was lost in the noise and Roody handed a cigar toward Eve before recognizing her in boots, britches, and flannel shirt.

Recognition came then and Roody made himself heard. "This is my hospitality car! Out! Out!" Roody crowded Eve back out on the platform.

Britt stepped between them.

Between her teeth Eve hissed, "Roody, you're a stinker!"

She stumbled backward down the caboose steps. Britt reached to keep her from falling and Roody leaned over the railing to yell after them, "There are ten trains going south from here this morning. Every one of them will be loaded from roof to rods. You'd better get aboard—your Pullman reservations are no good from here on!"

A switch engine whistled, backing to switch cars. The steam whistle, the grind of rolling coaches, bell clangor echoing from the freight yards sent Britt and Eve hurrying across the cindered grades.

It occurred to Britt that they had not seen the Casey gang in spite of Richter's prediction and as they worked through the crowd of humanity still trying to buy tickets he kept a sharp look-out. The sidings were lined with passenger coaches. Britt and Eve found the Pullman they had left an hour earlier and climbed aboard.

The berths had been made up. Every seat was full. Britt spied his seabag shoved under a seat, and decided to leave it there.

A waving arm caught their attention. It was Peardeedo, pointing to the place where he had put Eve's valise in the overhead rack. He was grinning and called to Eve, "This seat *junto a la ventana* I save for you!"

He vacated the seat, rising and backing out, hovered protectively over his guitar. Eve slid past the rugged, shaggy mustached man who occupied the seat by the aisle and sat down. Britt and Peardeedo stood in the aisle. The train jolted as engine and tender hooked up with jar, clank, and jerk.

"Where's Nate?" Eve asked Peardeedo.

"The *coche de la prensa, para los* reporters, it is first, behind the cars of baggage. *El padre* Quigley is with *Señor Richter*."

"Ministerial privilege," Eve winked at Britt.

The train backed through a switch, reversed with jarring shock, then pulled slowly forward past Roody's hospitality caboose. As the creaking wheels ground alongside the forward platform of the caboose, Britt saw the stylishly dressed Inez Basil.

Roody was reaching down to help her ascend the platform of the caboose.

"Roody and guests," Britt mused aloud, "a private car for the Oklahoma Run!"

The elderly man who sat beside Eve said, "Not quite. A lot of money was chipped in for that caboose. It's been setting there for a week, passing out cigars and beer to train crews. Anybody who wanted freight hauled in before the first southbound passenger train has been kicking in to the kitty. I kicked in some myself."

"We came from Wichita in this car last night," Eve said.

"I jus' stay on to hold a seat for my friend." Peardeedo smiled widely at Eve. "This conductor, he like you," he told Britt.

"You was lucky," the rugged man admitted.

Men were climbing the side of the slow-moving train now, struggling up onto the roof. The engine maneuvered through a second switch and began backing slowly. A shock of linkage carried up from the rear of the train.

"We've just picked up my influence-buying brother," Eve guessed. She turned to her seat mate to ask boldly, "Since you chipped in on it, why aren't you back in that caboose with them?"

A smile cut his sun-wrinkled face, "They're too pusillanimous for me, ma'am. That's why I ain't there. We might as well get acquainted. My name is Zack Hall."

The train eased past the Arkansas City depot, gathering speed as Eve introduced herself, Britt and Peardeedo, and they shook hands around.

Hall thrust a scuffed boot into the aisle, stretching his leg to extract a turnip watch from a tight pocket of pants made for horse riding.

"We got a three-hour ride ahead of us," he said settling back comfortably in the seat. "I been running a thousand head of cattle on leased government land about fifteen miles this side of Logan Station. This landrush sure has complicated things."

"*Pues*, now you have that to give away your land," Peardeedo said sympathetically.

"Not necessarily," Hall answered. "The Army made me trail my stock out. I sold some for Kansas City delivery, but I still got a good breeder herd stashed around on little bits of grass in the Cherokee Strip. We might get goin' again," Hall said optimistically.

Clear of the yards, the train rolled south through open country. It was brightly green, a spread of rolling earth with patches of blooming wild flowers, some areas dominated by a single color, others variegated with many colors.

"I got twenty-six cowboys ridin' in the race"—Hall stared far-eyed out across the rangeland—"tryin' to stake as many quarter sections as they can. Anything this side of the Cimarron. I figure to buy those boys' claims out, once they prove up."

"That's illegal," Eve accused.

"No, ma'am," Hall declared.

Mottes of cross-timbers blackjacks stood like islands across the broad prairies. The train wheels boomed hollowly crossing a trestle spanning a shallow pebbled water course.

Britt asked, "What if your twenty-six cowboys decide not to sell?"

"Their choice to make," Hall acceded. "Nothing I could do. But I ain't worrying. Them boys ain't sodbusters. They've been ridin' cowhands too long to get used to followin' along behind a horse rasslin' a plow."

The train's pace seemed measured and slow. An illusion, Britt thought, created by his own eagerness, and he speculated to Zack Hall, "Bad road bed?"

"No, no. It's new. We've had one hell of a lot of rain lately. But it's a good track. The fact is we got a speed limit set on us. We can't get to the unassigned land before noon, when the gun goes off." He grinned. "Think how them behind us feel. There'll be another trainload fifteen minutes behind us, an' it'll be like that all morning."

"*Porque—*" Peardeedo began, "for why we no see *la gente?* There are no people in this country."

"We'll be catching up with them pretty soon." Zack shook his head, "They was a slew of 'em cleared out of Ark City yesterday. From everywhere. Cleaned out the grocery and hardware stores. Fellow told me this mornin' you couldn't buy a shovel, a axe, or a bucket anywhere in town for love nor money. No flour, no eggs. Best business Ark City ever saw. Maybe the best they ever will see. Funny people, them Ark Citians. They cussed the boomers for bein' underfoot, but they shore did like all that business. Easter Sunday yesterday, an' they kep' the stores open all day."

The train rolled past the clapboard environs of Ponca Station. A shirt-sleeved, arm-gartered, eye-visored telegrapher stood outside the deserted station. He waved glumly, and Zack chuckled, "Shore is hell to be left behind out of all the doin's."

"This is supposed to be Indian Territory—where are all the Indians?" Eve asked.

"They been plaguin' the wagon trails," Zack said. "Them Poncas, carryin' rifles, they got no ca'tridges—but they look mean, grim as death. They ride from one settler camp to another, load up on handouts, then ride over the hill an' laugh like hell!" He chuckled again.

Two miles below Ponca Station the train rumbled over a long trestle. "This is Salt Fork trestle," Zack pointed out. "It's the one the newspapers been writin' about—the railroad bridge they planked over so the boomers could cross."

The steady rocking motion of the train and the dull wear of time were taking their toll. Standees had begun to sit on the floor of the aisle. Peardeedo sat down in the aisle, strumming his guitar idly passing the time.

Britt hunkered down beside the seat, then gave up and sat. Feeling drowsy, he leaned against the arm, and was still drowsing there when Eve began to shake his shoulder, saying urgently, "Britt!"

There was horror in her voice. Her face was pale, her eyes transfixed and wide. As he leaned toward her, the train pulled past it—not more than an arm's length outside the car window.

Swinging from the crosstree of a passing telegraph pole was the body of a hanged man. The unnatural posture, the head twisted aside grotesquely by the taut hang-rope, rough-shod feet pointing freakishly earthward, he had been a poor man, roughly clothed. Now he was turning slowly in the erratic wind current stirred by the running train.

Eve seemed unable to look away in the long moment as it passed behind.

Zack Hall came forth with a ghoulish chuckle. "You read the sign hanging on him?"

"Something about '*he WAS a Sooner*'—"

"Yup. An' the rest of it, '*if you ARE a Sooner quit your claim, before you WAS a Sooner, too.*' Don't let it bother you, little lady. Seems like hangin' is the only medicine that'll cure a thief."

"Look who's talking!" she accused. "You've got a whole army of cowboys out there being Sooners."

"No, ma'am," Zack denied. "They'll make the race fair an' square."

Hall reasoned stoutly: "Look here, missy. Who's got the best chance in this race? The boomers? They're all strangers who never saw this country before. My cowhands are better mounted. They've rode this country for years, and they know exactly where they're headed. We got an advantage all right, but my boys'll run fair. Not one of 'em will jump the gun."

Zack mused thoughtfully, "Maybeso them boys would have soonered claims if I'd asked 'em to. But askin' would stick in my craw. It'd rot out their respect for me. Besides," he chuckled, "there's nothin' them boys like more'n a hoss race. I'll give good odds they'll win every claim we've aimed for."

"Why aren't *you* riding?" Eve asked.

"Too old an' stove up for a hoss race, missy. I'm pushin' seventy."

Eve leaned back against the seat. The flurry of talk that had sprung up in the car as the train passed the lynched man subsided. Britt had seen hanged men, deserters swung from a ship's yardarm, a sight to which he knew he would never become accustomed, but he had learned to hold his tongue lest he reveal his own weakness.

Britt considered the ease with which Zack Hall had accepted the hanging, moving effortlessly from violent death to talk of the land race. Eve had changed the subject as readily as Hall and recalling her fury at Dink Casey in the St. Louis depot Britt forced himself to reject the passing thought that she was capable of joining a lynch mob and taking a hand in hauling on the rope.

She's not really mean, he thought, just hot tempered. And mischievous. He was speculating again on his own embarrassment that night beside her Pullman berth. What might have happened if he had accepted her invitation? What would have happened if he had started to crawl into that Pullman berth with her? He suspected that she would have howled for help, then thoroughly enjoyed his mortification.

Her complete unconcern at a mortified store clerk's embarrassment while she determinedly dressed herself in men's clothing came to mind, and Britt shook his head. There was no way of knowing what she would do. She refused to conform to any social decorum of which she disapproved.

She had a way of revealing Roody at his shameful worst. Britt's contemplation was interrupted by Zack Hall's laconic announcement:

"Yonder's the line."

8

The interior of the car was vibrant, instantly alert. Men in the aisle scrambled erect. Stretching across the horizon to infinity Britt saw a rising line of dust.

Lifting like a theater curtain, the thinning flimsy gauze of dust revealed the spread of prairie. Zack Hall stretched to have out his turnip watch.

"Twelve-ten. The gun went off at noon. We're right behind."

The train penetrated the dust, a red haze through which the train passed slowly.

Beyond the line, where the waiting boomers had churned the prairie, the April earth lay greening and no dust lifted. The rising cloud fell behind drifting northward on the apparently gentle southerly wind.

The train began an almost steady whistle hooting. It caught and passed the most laggardly of the boomer wagons, a decrepit rig with soiled and flapping wagon sheets. At the pace of the train the crude lettering painted on the wagon's side was readable: CHINCH BUGGED IN ARKANSAS—DROUTHED OUT IN KANSAS—OKLAHOMA HERE WE COME.

The train pulled close alongside another dry-boarded rickety wagon with wobbling wheels. On one side of the wagon tongue a mule was hitched. On the other side the settler himself was hitched and tugging at a singletree. The boomer's dyspeptic wife perched on the seat of the slow-moving wagon, a cob pipe in her toothless gums.

Zack Hall laughed, "He needs a partner with one mule and no wagon."

Farther ahead the quality of the rigs improved. Britt saw new Studebaker wagons running hard and steadily, with bows and wagon sheet removed to lessen wind resistance. Some of these wagons were carrying families, with dogs running alongside. Others hauled loads of male adults, their families left behind until they had claims staked. Some wagons carried equipment, new sod-breaking plows with rodded moldboards.

One wagon followed a pack of lean hunting hounds that ranged far out ahead. The settler and his wife rode the bounding spring seat of the plunging wagon. A jumble of children peered out through the curved semicircle of wagon sheet over the tailgate. The settler hauled reins trying to slow the wagon as it descended a sharp incline into a gulley and the children disappeared, shaken down into the wagon bed.

The settler whipped up his team to climb the ascending bank and a harness tug snapped. The wagon tongue dropped, spearing the brow of the dry wash and the covered wagon slewed, upending with slow and heavy movement to crash on the emerging crest.

As the view of the wrecked wagon passed behind the train the horses were still struggling and entangled in the harness and children were crawling into sight from beneath the overturned wagon's bows.

As the settler and wife came climbing out, dazedly, Hall said, "Lucky. He might of killed somebody. Oughta gone around that gulley."

"*Gente estúpida!*" Peardeedo murmured. "Hurrys make waste."

Britt's own tiredness began disappearing in rising excitement as the steady moving train began overtaking lighter vehicles in the vanguard of the land rush, buggies, surreys, buckboards, a racing cart with pacer hitched, its goggled, cloth-capped driver urging his trotter near a horseman riding fast and low in his saddle. All across the prairie now dismounted men were waving flags and driving stakes to claim land across which stampeding riders still charged.

"There'll be some contested claims here," Zack Hall predicted.

They were overtaking the fastest runners now. Hall's voice rose as he declared, "There's one of my boys—Stub Riley. He's cutting off the quarter north of the Cimarron's Big Bend. That quarter's got a spring on it. Go after it, Stub," Hall yelled as if the rider could hear him.

The long-reaching horse and ripple-shirted Stub Riley moved as a single creature. The train drew even and passed. Riley became a speck riding hellbent for the southeast horizon. On the far side of the train aisle someone shouted.

Britt crouched to look out through the far window. A quarter mile out across the land two men afoot were circling each other.

The pair of men with upraised fists circled warily. Their body punches hit forearms and elbows or swung short and their wary circling began again.

Zack Hall said, "Don't look like anybody's going to get hurt there."

As Britt last saw the pair they were still circling like prize fighters, feinting and ducking. The train was outrunning the fastest riders.

Peardeedo predicted gleefully, "We're going to get there first."

"I knew we'd pass the most," Hall said. A horse ain't a machine. Flesh an' bone gets tired."

The train ran downslope through thick-growing brush into the Cimarron Valley. Red sandstone bluffs interrupted to the west. Eastward the vista flattened. From the alluvial river bottom belly high stands of buffalo grass bent with the wind. The shallow Cimarron glistened in narrowing curve around the sandstone bluffs.

Turning south and west in bending arcs, twisting sinuously among wide sand bars, the river was a shining silver ribbon set sparkling by the nooning sun. From a thicket of salt cedar in the flat a group of horsemen burst out.

Three at first, then others and Britt counted eleven in all riding hard across the sand bar. It was like a magician's illusion. Britt had not seen them enter the thicket, but far out in front of any other rider, their emergence was tangible enough. Their horses were lathered and shiny with sweat.

Zack Hall watched them, solemnly and vigilant. "I'd venture a guess," he said flatly. "The lather on them horses is saddle soap!"

"They washed their horses?" Peardeedo asked, incredulous.

"They want to look like they have been runnin' hard and long," Hall said. "That's a bunch of Sooners. They've been hid out in that brush all night."

Hall watched the horsemen with intensity as they made tracks across the river-rippled sand bar. Their horses reached the river, cleaving into it, sending up showers of cascading water as they crossed the knee-deep stream. "If you see one of them in court contestin' somebody's claim you'll know how to testify."

The horsemen took the bank in running jumps, hoofs jarring clumps of sod into the current, and disappeared in tall cedars that guarded the Cimarron's south bank.

Eve slid to the edge of the cushioned seat. The train boomed onto the Cimarron River trestle. Telegraph poles alongside the network of bridge timbers seemed squatters. The wires strung on their crosstrees made low clearance above the coach roofs.

Britt remembered those who had climbed on the train roof at Arkansas City half expecting to see some scraped off. The long trestle spanned the sandy flats to reach the ballasted embankment. The coaches negotiating the gradual curve bent through a scattering of section hands' quarters lining the approach to Logan Station.

Eve twisted to face the partly opened car window and hoisted it wide open. A gust of smoky air swept into the car and the train slowed perceptibly. A work train on siding and a group of section hands stood watching the arriving train. Holding or leaning on pickaxes and shovels all seemed to wait poised, in attitudes of anticipation.

East of the creeping train a clutter of station buildings and the depot water tank initiated a scattering of structures cresting the east rising slope. Men were beginning to spill off the train.

A thousand yards east a two-story frame building on the hill-crest stood alone among a few tents. Before the two-story building an American flag on a crooked blackjack staff fluttered out stiffly in the south wind.

The clamor in the car was noisy. The scrape of heels as men slid down the roof, scuffing roughly against the side of the car in leaping off came then.

Scattering, stumbling, running, shrugging bundles across shoulders, heaving at luggage, grasping blanket rolls as they ran, men went in spreading swarm up the east rising slope. Eve was out of her seat.

The train still rolled, slowing, grinding, screeching.

Eve said, "Bring my valise. I'm going to stake a lot!"

She climbed out through the open window legs first as Britt reached to grab her disappearing arm.

He missed.

Her fingers were visible for an instant clinging to the window sill. Britt leaned and fell across the startled rancher who grunted at the impact of Britt's weight. Her fingers were gone from the sill.

Britt saw her fall tumbling along the ballast, then she was up swiping at a cinder-scraped and bleeding cheek. She arm-waved in beckoning haste to Britt and ran up the slope.

Britt thrust himself erect cursing, shoving aside men who crowded the aisle, leaning to peer through each window as he passed, then remembered Eve's valise in the overhead luggage rack.

He shouldered his way back, pulled down the valise, heaved his seabag from beneath the seat where it had been stowed, and piled them in the seat beside the brown-paper-wrapped store parcel.

"There she goes!" Zack Hall pointed upslope toward Eve who ran darting through the herd of boomers swarming over the hillside.

"Throw that stuff to me," Britt ordered and jammed his upper body out through the small window.

Reaching to seize the ledge along the top of the car he swung out, and dropped. He had one final glimpse of Peardeedo trying to protect his guitar among the tangle of men trying to climb out the windows or shoving ruthlessly toward the exits. All of the train's creeping length was alive with boomers hurdling from windows, from exit vestibules, coach roofs, launching themselves out from the rods underneath the coaches in disregard of still rolling wheels. Eve's valise came sailing out the window.

Britt ran alongside to snatch it up, then on toward the seabag which bounded down the slope farther ahead. The parcel came last, bursting its wrapping on impact. Britt crammed Eve's dress and his uniform blouse back into the torn package as his eyes swept the hillside, trying to locate her.

She was gone. With a final squeal of protest the train came to a full stop, the last car a hundred feet down the track from where Britt stood. Men still leaped down and away from the train but the mass of them were churning up the hillside like the retreating surf of a tidal wave.

Britt shouldered the seabag, locked the parcel beneath his arm, juggled for a grip on the handle of the valise and followed for three short steps, then stopped.

Instead, he went to the end car, stacked seabag, package, and valise against the rails of its platform, and began climbing. He swung aloft on the car's ladder and scrambled onto the roof of the car.

Here he stood collecting his wits, then began a meticulous eye search of the mass of humanity flowing over the crest of the first rise. The land dipped down there then began another rise, peaking out after a thousand yards to hide an indefinite distance from his view. The land came in sight again on a far, gradual incline, toward distant heights, lying in long green rolls like a gentle sea, toward horizon and infinity.

Along the first slope claimants now perched on steep lots beside driven stakes. Tents were already beginning to spring up, taking shape like wind filling sails. Here and there, pairs and groups of men disputed with violently outflung gestures, pointing, claiming, and disclaiming in heated argument, debating who stopped first on the lot. Some stood statue-like in determination to remain immovable where they had taken their stand.

The retreating line still moved ahead, dispersing and thinning as men stopped to drive their stakes and make claim. From atop the caboose Britt could now see a tortuous line of men beginning to form, stringing downhill from the two-story frame structure before which the flag blew stiffly. Eve, in her britches and shirt, could be among the men forming that line. It was impossible to recognize any individual at that distance.

Then some style of movement of one of the toy figures caught his eye. Britt studied it in concentration. It was, he was sure, a female in britches and shirt, but then the figure's tiny upraised arm held an object which in the distance appeared to be a rifle. Eve had carried no rifle.

Britt exhaled in disgust and surrendered. He gave a moment's attention to his own surroundings. On the freight dock just beyond the depot small groups of men searched frantically through stacks of stockpiled freight, seeking their property from the vast accumulation there; crates, boxes, barrels. Some were marked boldly in green, red, blue, vivid hues and patterns painted to facilitate quick identification.

There was no mistaking the wig-like carrot hair bursting out below the derby of one man among the groups who prowled the freight heaps in running haste. It was Roody. Britt stood in the ear-whistling wind that blew hard and steady across the top of the car and stared at him.

The wind carried snatches of muffled shouts. It whipped Britt's clothing. The engine bell began to clang, irregularly, as though tired. The train gave a lurch, then stopped again. Britt paused to watch the wild gesticulations of Roody's attempt to direct a pair of helpers in searching through the accumulation of freight on the Santa Fe dock.

The train began to move, inching ahead to clear the track for the next section due to follow in from Arkansas City in minutes. Britt rode, leaning against the wind as the locomotive pulled ahead, until he was even with the depot. Then he swung down from the roof to kick the valise, seabag, and parcel out on the slowly passing freight dock. Britt jumped off after them, timing his departure to bring him up even with Roody and the pair of crate-hoisting men.

Roody jerked off his derby. His hair sprung out like released stiff wire as he mopped his sweating face with a work-dirted hand. "Give us a hand here, Britt. We've found the wall sections, but they're wedged in—we sure can use another pair of shoulders. Here, boys, move aside a little. Make room for the lieutenant and I'll grab—"

Roody stopped short to stare when Britt did not move. His sweaty face turned angry and pugnacious. "Hell's fire, man! Grab hold! We've got to have this building up and the safe set in before dark—"

Britt stepped to grab Roody's lapel. He shook him roughly and said, "Listen to me. Your sister is somewhere up on that hill. She's alone. She's done a damn fool thing. But let's have you show some sense."

Roody struck Britt's hand away. He was near hysteria, his glance rolling walleyed as he sought to observe what his helpers were doing. His spasm of jerked-out words were insensible as he spun away, butting his shoulder against the slats of a wooden crate. "Prize up there, fellow! If we can break out the floor joist—" he grunted, lifting with frantic effort.

Britt stepped away, soberly considering what he must do. He

looked about, speculating on where he might leave his seabag, Eve's valise, and the parcel. There was no place so he retrieved all three, juggling them to distribute their weight as equally as possible, shouldering the seabag, the valise in hand, the parcel beneath his arm.

Circling the depot he avoided a running man and commenced a slanting trek up the hill. Everyone was running, singly, in pairs, in groups. Britt walked, watching light runners, heavy runners, running fast, slow, or jogging. A pair carrying freight ran awkwardly, panting and struggling as they wrestled their load.

A bunch of five toughs, lugging a huge roll of brown tent canvas like carnival roustabouts, labored up the grade trying to run and treadmilling, frustrating their own progress with the bulky load. Britt set his course slightly north by east, toward the hilly place where he had last seen Eve.

The second train rolled grinding in, huffing, with clanging bell. Britt heard its backing steam resisting the engine drivers as it slowed to half beneath the depot water tank. Newcomers from its coaches were already swarming up the hill.

Taking his bearings from the blackjack flagstaff before the frame building to his right Britt kept his eyes sorting the farrago swirling around him. He changed course at the spot where he had seen Eve in his last glimpse of her from the train, turning and heading straight upslope.

He was beginning to perspire under his load. The warmth of the early afternoon sun bore down hard from a cloudless sky. The wave of men from the second train still charged past him and Britt slowed in their backwash. An angry sense welled up in him.

The second train had doubled the human swarm he had to search through. When the third train arrived the problem would be tripled. Before the afternoon was over there would be ten trains. Britt felt an impulse to hurry.

Everywhere around him people were running, erratically,

frantically. The thought that every fifteen minutes, each arriving train, multiplied his problem, sent urgent juices into his muscles. But the sight of the tag-end stragglers pumping past him up the hill steadied his impulses. Britt could envision himself searching in indirection, missing areas, doubling back to search areas already covered, and he deliberately slowed his steady walk to be certain of carefully scrutinizing every human in range of his vision.

Men on horseback were beginning to mingle with lot seekers on foot. Britt remembered the fast riders the train had passed just before crossing the Cimarron, and he felt new dismay at the swelling of the crowd. Horsemen riding into Logan Station to seek town lots, instead of staking claims outside the town, added to his irritation, then he became amused at his own senseless resentment.

But more passengers on every arriving train, more boomers coming in on horseback, in wagons—by every conveyance except angels' wings, Britt thought, there'll be ten thousand people here by nightfall. Britt kept his eyes prying at the restless, growing, hurrying, shifting human swarm. This is futile, he thought, then the set of shoulders of a distant horseman caught his eye. Something about the shape of the young rider, his manner of sitting his saddle, drew Britt's full attention.

Light vehicles had begun to mingle among the confusion. Buggies, surreys, buckboards, light drays drawn by horses reeking hot and sweaty from the drive. Britt scowled thoughtfully at the back of the faraway rider who had drawn his attention, worrying at the recollection and wondering why, as the young horseman broke his horse into a gallop.

Then in instant vision like a fading photograph his mind called up the set of young Dink Casey's shoulders as the horse he rode double with the outlaw Soldier Jack had bounded off into the Missouri timber the night of the attempted train robbery. The distant horseman Britt watched now was suddenly gone, lost in the far crowd. Britt still stood, fixed and thoughtful.

If that was Dink Casey . . . if Casey encountered Eve . . . if he were to take her, and harm her . . . skylined against the slope another tableau caught Britt's eye.

A Sibley tent stood glistening in bleached white newness. Its irregular shape against the sky was filled slatting and snapping in the crisp wind. Before it posed two men, one sitting on the campstool, the other standing with a high-booted foot on his partner's stool. Both men were neatly dressed and darkly bearded.

Both were armed with holstered pistols and .44 caliber rifles. A lettered banner stretched in front of the tent stated THIS LOT IS CLAIMED. KEEP OFF THE GRASS. Both wore white pith helmets, giving them the incongruent look of explorers camped on African veldt.

Downhill a photographer had erected a heavy tripod and camera and was huddled beneath its black covering cloth, recording their motionless image for posterity. Other than Britt, the passing rush ignored the odd tableau as if it did not exist.

Britt turned down the opposite side of the slope and dismissed the muffled clanging bell and tooting whistle from the depot as unimportant. He could not recall whether this was the arrival of the third or the fourth train.

He thought momentarily of the emigrant car with its load of crusading W.C.T. "ewes." The emigrant car had not been a part of the first train. He had not seen it among the coaches of the second train as he had watched it pulling in. Britt reached the bottom of the hill, where the land leveled for a distance then resumed its upward grade. He stopped to consider.

Facing the pale blue-white of the distant horizon he watched the swirling activity of the steadily increasing number of claim seekers.

Would Eve have continued on toward the edge of all this activity, toward what would eventually be the edge of town? Or would she have turned back to try to stake a lot nearer what would be the center of town? Britt concluded that she would want to be in the center. He swung south for a hundred yards then turned back uphill, toward the direction of the depot.

The seabag on his right shoulder had become a leaden weight. His left arm, with the parcel locked beneath it, was numb from shoulder to fingers. Clothing bulged from the torn parcel. Britt stopped and set the valise on the ground.

The brown-paper parcel was wet with perspiration. A force five wind blew across the slope and as he stood, the evaporation of his own sweat created an illusion of coolness in the stiff wind. Britt lowered his seabag, stuffed the clothing back in the torn parcel as best he could, picked up seabag and valise and went on.

He could no longer continue in a straight course. Horsemen and vehicles, even heavy spring wagons, came plunging through the crowd as if they were driven on open prairie.

Look out and mind your footwork or you'll be run down, he thought. Tents were going up everywhere, indiscriminate of location. Some town, he thought, no streets had been marked off and half-erected tents littered the ground leaving no room for streets.

Blowing loose canvas whipped in the wind as settlers tried to anchor it with stakes, and as more and more were successful Britt found himself unable to see around the erected tents. Frustration oppressed him and his search became less methodical.

Roody was right. There was no choice but to abandon Eve to her own willfulness. Her voice came at him from the side, shrill and hysterical—

"Sir—sir—"

Britt spun around, dropping the luggage and using his sleeve to swab away the perspiration that ran down into his eyes.

It was not Eve.

The approaching woman wore a heavy, dark, ankle-length dress. It was dusty and torn. Her hair, in long strands blown loose from her hat, whipped across her face. She clawed at her hair with raking fingers, dragging her hat loose from its hat pins.

Her clawing nails scratched her forehead and the wounds oozed pinkly. She stared at Britt with the same glazed stare Britt had seen in Roody's eyes as he had worked frantically at the pile of freight at the depot.

As the woman's fingers clutched Britt's arm her white eyes fled up and around without pause and unseeing.

"Sir—" her voice keened like the wind. "Have you seen my husband?"

Her eyes fled again in unfocused fear. Her breath was constricted and came in tired, heaving gusts.

Britt, in quiet calm, said, "Madam, I don't know your husband."

"Yes," she said vaguely and Britt knew she had not heard his reply, "we were together until the train came—then somehow—"

Britt gripped both her shoulders, "Madam, listen to me—"

"I've lost him—somehow—in this crowd." Her glance lit briefly on his face. "No, you're not—have you seen my husband—I've been looking—"

"Listen to me," Britt insisted. "Where—"

"Everywhere," she interrupted. Distraught, unable even to co-ordinate her eyes with the direction she was pointing she said tiredly, "I've looked—" Her glance wandered back to Britt.

Gently, Britt forced her down until she sat upon the seabag and knelt in front of her. The hard grip of his hands held her as her eyes fled again then came to focus on his gripping hands.

"I don't know your husband, ma'am," Britt said firmly. "If I were you I'd return to the depot. He'll likely go there to look for you."

"The depot. Yes, the depot—" She lurched against his hand to rise, looking off in the direction opposite from the depot.

Britt held her fast. "The depot is to your right, ma'am."

The hard, unyielding grip of his hands restrained her and seemed to sink more deeply into her consciousness. She looked for a moment directly into his face. Tears formed and brimmed in her eyes. She fumbled to remove a handkerchief from her purse and wipe away the tears.

"The depot," Britt said again, "is the one certain point in this unorganized place. Your husband would expect you to return there and wait for him. There's a depot agent there. Your husband may already have returned there to inquire of the agent, or to leave word where he can be found."

The solid patience of Britt's voice seemed to undergird her strength. She became calm, and was able to give him a smile though it trembled and quivered, and the welling tears still flowed.

"Yes," she said. "I understand."

Britt felt that she did. "If I were you," he repeated calmly, "I'd go to the depot. Wait there at least through the afternoon. Where are you from?"

"Wichita," she said, gaining control. "My husband hoped to claim a lot. He is a jeweler, and we felt that we might—" She hesitated, faltering.

"Do you have some money?" Britt asked.

She looked confused, then comprehended, "Oh. You mean with me? Yes." She felt for the purse that hanging from her elbow had swung almost behind her.

Britt suggested, "There will certainly be a train returning north sometime this evening. If your husband doesn't locate you, perhaps you should return to Wichita."

"Of course," she said. "I should have thought of the depot." She now seemed only embarrassed, and looked directly at his hands gripping her shoulders. "I am all right now. Thank you."

Britt released her and she stood.

"Thank you," she said again. Her eyes were reddened from the tears. Glancing up, she lowered her face at once. "I am ashamed of having lost control so badly." She reached to grasp the fullness of her skirt for walking, and turned toward the depot.

Britt watched her moving purposefully up the hill, and gave passing thought to the chance that Eve might have returned to the depot. He discarded that possibility—her least probable act would be something that might be helpful to someone worrying about her safety.

The vision of the distraught woman returned to his thoughts. Britt recalled Roody's hysteria, and Eve was Roody's sister. If it were a family trait—the thought that she might finally realize that she was alone, that she might lose her equilibrium, that she might be searching for help among these crazy running boomers. Britt remembered Eve's flight from the train and that she had fallen. Her face was bleeding when he last saw her. Doggedly he loaded himself and started up the hill.

9

With the exertion of climbing Britt was sweating again. He became increasingly conscious of thirst. The tumult of arrival, and losing Eve, his encounter with Roody, then the hysterical woman, had combined in an excitement so absorbing it had shut out any thoughts of self.

But now his thirstiness grew so extreme that it was difficult to think of anything else. It occurred to Britt that since his cup of coffee at breakfast he had had no water, no liquid at all. The day's excitement and steady perspiring had dehydrated him. His thirst became incredible, physically painful. Britt forced himself to imagine Eve in dire straits in order to fix his attention on the search for her. Climbing the hill he reached the center of town. Streets had been surveyed and marked off here and he found himself surprised at how much order had begun to emerge.

Britt glanced up at the sun and was even more surprised to note how far it had traveled since he had left the train. It was approaching midafternoon. The day was wearing out. So was he. This hilltop area no longer resembled a hive of disorderly ants. Horsemen and vehicles moved in the lanes that had been laid out and staked off as streets.

In the lots along the street progress had been made. Tents were up—large ones. A sizable wooden sign leaned against one: HALE, HALE, AND CROW—LAND ATTY'S.

On the adjoining lot a billowing canvas sign the size of a carnival banner proclaimed:

G. CARTER, MEDICAL DOCTOR

PHYSICIAN AND SURGEON

SPECIALIST

CURES GUARANTEED

Chronic, Female, and Skin Diseases, Catarrh

Resident Physician, not a Traveling Doctor

TESTIMONIALS

There were columns of testimonials. Britt was so thirsty now he felt sick enough without reading the symptoms of others' ailments. He paused in front of the two-story frame building at the crest of the hill, the building he had seen from the roof of the train. Its sign read GOVERNMENT LAND OFFICE.

No longer standing lonely and alone on a bare hilltop, the building was now the center of all activity. Its flag snapped briskly from the crooked blackjack flagstaff. Boomers lined up seeking to register their claims stretched in a curving line for two-hundred yards down the street. A street gambler had set up his kiester and was working the long line.

"Are you all down?" chanted the gambler.

He dealt a layout of three-card monte on top of the kiester, chanting, his voice carrying, "We have a winner. Five dollars to the gent in the canary-striped galluses. Lay your bets, gentlemen. Don't be pikers. Are you all down—"

Britt saw her.

He walked a few yards farther for a look across the shoulders of the line of waiting boomers. Eve sat alone, cross-legged and morose, in the center of the lot two claims downhill from the land office.

Britt tried to swallow. His throat was too dry. He cut through the line, across the lots, and directly to her.

Eve looked up. Her face brightened. "Hello," she said.

Britt dumped the valise, parcel, and seabag on the ground in front of her.

She cocked her knees up and locked her arms around them. Rocking back, she beamed, "I got a good one, didn't I?"

Britt kept silent.

Her brightness ebbed. "It hasn't done any good. I can't do anything about it."

Britt's muscles began to tremble. He would like to have thought it was tiredness but he knew it was anger.

Morose again, Eve lamented, "If I get in that line, somebody'll jump it."

"What?" Britt felt both irritated and confused.

"Jump my claim," she explained, then brightened once more. "You go get in line!"

"Hellsfire!"

Eve looked at him in amazement.

Britt asked tersely, "Have you given any thought to where you're going to sleep tonight?"

She said frankly, "No. Have you?"

"It's no problem for me. Some settler will let me sleep under his wagon box."

She said coyly, "I'm with you," and looked up at him through her eyelashes.

In the strained silence, the conversation from the claim adjoining, downhill toward the depot, drifted up to them. Two men were on the claim, one unloading groceries from a light wagon and stacking them beneath a taut-stretched tent fly. The other was saying, "You wouldn't consider selling?"

The other replied shortly, "No!"

"Well," the hopeful buyer sounded apologetic. He carried the same heavy tripoded camera that Britt had seen set up and photographing the pith-helmeted claim holders earlier in the afternoon.

Eve shouted, "Hey! Mister!"

The photographer turned toward them. Britt remembered the pin-striped pants legs he had seen protruding below the black camera cloth.

Eve asked, sly with caution, "You want to buy a claim?"

"Yes, ma'am." Still apologetic, the photographer came up the hill toward them. "I was so busy taking pictures I got left out. I've a helper down there"—he indicated a wagon stopped at the edge of what would be the street—"I need to get a dark room set up—"

Eve interrupted. "What'll you offer?"

"For this claim?" The apologetic photographer stared at Eve's shirt and pants in some confusion, then looked away. "I guess I'm not used to doing business with a wo— a lady. What will you take?"

"One hundred dollars," Eve said briskly.

His face lightened with a pleasure that indicated he had expected to be asked more. "Done!"

Eve offered her hand. Instead of shaking hands he dug for his wallet, and carefully counted green-backed currency into her extended hand.

Eve folded the money. "You're lucky. There have been a dozen claim jumpers on this lot. I told every one of them where to go!"

"And I appreciate it, ma'am. This is a better location than I would have secured if I'd claimed a lot as soon as I got off the train." The photographer waved at his assistant. "Drive 'er on up here, Calvin."

Eve picked up the brown-wrapped parcel. "Now I'm solvent," she declared. "Come on."

"Come on where?" Britt asked.

"Anywhere! I'm tired of sitting. Let's go see what's going on."

"I haven't been sitting." Britt toed the seabag, rolling it across the grassy sod. "I've seen what's going on. What happened to the cut on your face?"

"What cut?"

"When you jumped off the train. Your cheek was bleeding."

"I didn't cut my face. My hand got skinned on the cinders. The blood on my cheek was from trying to rub the dirt off my face. I got a boomer to give me a chaw of tobacco—held it against the scratch on my hand. It's not even sore now."

Eve took a wadded, wrinkled handkerchief from her pants pocket. "I couldn't find any water to wash my face. Had to use my own spit. Which reminds me, I'm out of spit now. I'm thirsty!"

Britt nodded. His mouth felt as parched and dry as sun-weathered wood.

"Let's go down to the depot," Eve suggested, "and pull down the spout of the Santa Fe water tank. I could drink it dry!"

Britt bent to hoist the seabag.

"Wait a minute," Eve said guardedly.

Britt followed her eyes across the street. A boyish-appearing youth there stood confronted by a voluble arm-waving talker. The talker, well larded with fat, wore a baggy white suit and a Panama hat. Beside the talker a more powerful man stood, rough-clothed, his pants stuffed inside high boots, his broad chest framed by wide suspenders. His belt sagged, suspending a holstered revolver.

The fat man's motioning arms were clearly ordering the young man off the claim, and the youth's mild negative headshake incited his baggy white-suited opponent to vehement anger. Britt observed that the roughly dressed man was easing his gun out of the holster.

Britt thought grimly, here I go again, inviting myself into something that is none of my business. The gun was out now, but it was not yet possible to determine the gunman's intention—to use his weapon as a threat or in some more lethal way. Determinedly overcoming the tremors of fear that rose in him Britt walked across the street.

As he arrived behind the gunman it was apparent the man intended to use the gun as a club. He was dropping his arm back gaining momentum to strike when Britt touched his shoulder and said, "I wouldn't."

The man swung to face Britt then both the gunman and the

baggy-suited fat man turned toward the commotion Eve made as she ran onto the lot. Britt could almost feel the muzzle of the gun which was now aimed at his brisket.

Eve still carried the brown-wrapped parcel and she hurled it, hitting the gunman square in the chest. The tear that had opened when the parcel was tossed from the train burst wide open. Clothing exploded from the bundle, scattering in the wind and draping the gunman and the fat man.

Britt's uniform, Eve's dress and her underwear caught on the pair's clothing. Whipped in the breeze, a lacy garment hung on the gunman's arm then blew loose. Clothing was blowing all over the town lot claim.

The excitement had not gone unnoticed by the long line of boomers that extended from the land office down the hill toward the depot. Their laughter had begun when the bundle exploded. It increased as Eve began running around the lot gathering the blowing garments.

The white-suited fat man ordered, "Matt, holster your gun." Huffing and snorting to maintain pompous dignity he boomed, directing his question at Britt:

"Sir, do you know who I am?"

Eve paused in her gathering to shout: "Is there any reason we ought to know?"

"I am Quentin Nash, attorney-at-law, representing Colonel Lemuel Hampton of the L. S. & W. stage line."

Eve snatched up the lace-trimmed slip that had blown from the gunman's arm. "Who's your tame wolf?"

The gunman growled, "I ain't so tame—"

The blustering attorney silenced him with a gesture. "This, madam," he said fulsomely, "is Matt Lang, frontiersman and plains guide for Colonel Hampton."

Eve gripped her underwear in doubled fists. She bristled in the gunman's face, "Well, guide yourself off and bully someone else before I beat you to death with my brassiere!"

Lang reached for her arm. Britt stepped between them to shove and the gunman stumbled backward. The boyish youth whose contested claim had started the encounter moved in to grab the gunman's arms and pin them behind him. He made a good try but Lang was too powerful for him. With grunt and shove he broke away and again drew his revolver.

This time the baggy-suited lawyer Nash stepped in to touch Lang's gun barrel with his hand urging, "Come, Matt, let's have no street brawl . . ." His hissed caution—something about a thousand witnesses—reached Britt's ears as Nash again raised his voice to declare, "Remember the colonel will be a man of standing in this community."

With a resigned shrug of frustrated anger Matt Lang holstered the gun and stalked off the lot with lawyer Nash hurrying to fall in beside him.

Left were Britt, Eve, and the young man whose face was flushed red from the attempt to pinion Lang. With beads of sweat from the effort standing out on his forehead, he grinned with relief.

"Whew!" he exhaled, and looked at Eve. "Little Miss Dynamite. I'm Joel Decatur."

Britt shook hands. "A familiar name. Any connection with the commodore?"

Still grinning, young Decatur said, "No. So far as I know. Just a coincidence of name."

"I'm Britt Pierce, lieutenant U.S.N."

Decatur nodded. "I can see why you'd be interested in that name. I appreciate both of you interceding in my behalf."

"No problem," Eve declared. "I was bored. All we had to postpone was going after a drink of water."

"I am about to expire from thirst, too." Decatur, surely no more than twenty, tugged the collar of his neat white shirt, thrusting out his tongue and bugging his eyes in a caricature of extreme thirst.

Britt noted that Eve was admiring young Decatur's blond handsomeness.

She said, "We were heading for the water tank at the depot."

Joel laughed. "That was empty an hour ago. We're surrounded by thirsty boomers." His face, a rare perfection of features, was so warmly friendly that his handsomeness was inoffensive. "The nearest water is the river. I've got a bucket. Hold this claim for me and I'll walk to the river for water."

As Decatur, carrying his bucket, walked off toward the river, three men came from the land office carrying chain, stake, and transit. They hurried eastward, down the far side of the slope. Britt sat down, straddling his seabag, enjoying the chance to rest.

Eve held the gathered clothing she had retrieved. "What'll I do with this?"

He looked for the torn remains of the paper bundle. It was useless trash blowing across the lot. "Here," he said, shoving Eve's valise toward her. "Give me my uniform."

While she repacked her valise he stowed his uniform in the seabag.

Eve walked about the lot, observing the activity around them. She watched the three-man surveying crew disappear in the crowd and called to Britt, "What was that all about?"

"I expect they'll extend the street surveys east. Whoever laid out this town planned for about half this many people. There are no streets, or lot surveys, beyond the foot of that hill."

"It's a mess, isn't it?" Eve sat down, tailor fashion, on the ground.

Across the street in front of a large tent with outstretched fly a heavy freight wagon drawn by six spans of steaming, tired mules, came to a halt. The mule skinner dropped the tailgate noisily and began unloading a grocery stock with the help of an aproned grocer.

Eve watched the green eye-shaded grocer and the mule skinner then declared, "That's going to be a store." She was up and leaving the lot. "I'm going grocery buying. If we wait till he puts up his sign we won't be able to get in there."

Britt started up, "Let me—"

"You bought breakfast," she yelled back. "This is on me."

She was back in fifteen minutes with a filled bag. "I had to use my powers of persuasion," she snickered, "but—" She began to display her purchases: canned peaches, dried beef, canned tomatoes, a container of hardtack, and a sack of hard candy.

Eve knelt on the ground and wedged a can of peaches between her knees. "Have you got a jackknife?"

Britt saw the four men come riding over the hill, past the land office. Two rode together behind the lead rider. The fourth came along behind in the manner of a lone rear guard. They rode well spaced apart, looking everything over carefully, passing the lengthening line of boomers that angled crookedly down the hill.

The rider in the lead was the shaggy-haired boy who had attempted the train holdup.

In the noisy confusion that continued to accompany the birth of Logan Station, a remarkable hush was falling along the path of the four riders. Of the pair following the boy, the nearest rider looked old, a man prematurely aged. He rode with a tired sagging posture, his whiskery, worry-lined face pointed straight ahead.

The rider beside him had a small head atop a big body. His face was small featured and mean and he rode with a ferret-eyed interest in all his surroundings, missing nothing. Britt noted that his arm was bandaged and carried awkwardly, his hand resting uncomfortably on the saddle horn.

The silence that fell before the riders remained in their wake. Some among the crowd in the street and in the waiting line of boomers obviously knew the four men. Their silence was imitated by others, probably in curiosity, but it created an over-all effect of awe.

The fourth rider, tall and cadaverous, was not impassive. He rode smiling, bitterly and cynically, wearing a near derisive sneer that dominated his long face. He rode swinging his head from side to side in arrogance, as if challenging anyone in the crowd to challenge him.

As the quiet fell the crowd's wary observance caught Eve's attention. She looked up toward the street and the four riders, forgetting the can of peaches held between her knees.

"The Caseys?" she asked boldly.

Eve did not whisper, and her question was sharp and loud in the stillness. It drew the attention of shaggy Dink Casey, riding in the lead. He turned in his saddle to stare directly at her.

"Dink, Bulldog, Bung, and Soldier Jack," Britt said, recalling Peardeedo's rhyming parody. The rider with the wounded arm must be the one he had hit with his second shot during the attempted raid on the train, Britt guessed.

Britt wished for the Navy Colt, buried somewhere deep in his seabag, and abandoned that thought. It would take too long to find it.

Eve said flatly, "Why doesn't someone arrest them? Aren't they bandits?"

She returned Dink Casey's stare coldly, and he turned and looked away. Eve locked eyes then with the arrogant Soldier Jack Hickey, who rode rear guard.

Soldier Jack lifted his reins and swung his horse to ride onto the claim. Bulldog Casey, hearing the horse behind him turn, glanced over his shoulder. "Let's ride on, Jack," he said.

Hickey accepted the command reluctantly, without altering the snarl on his saturnine face he straightened his horse. The four rode on down the hill toward the depot.

Britt considered the possibility that the Caseys had not recognized them. Eve certainly had not been wearing men's clothes during the incident in the St. Louis depot. He had been in uniform at the encounter on the train. Dink Casey had even mentioned the uniform, insisting that he'd remember Britt's brass buttons.

But Britt recalled how long Dink Casey had stared him full in the face as Casey lay outstretched in the emigrant car's aisle.

Long enough for Casey to have fixed Britt's features in his mind. And Dink Casey's revenge threat had hardly sounded like idle talk.

"They're bandits, aren't they?" Eve insisted. "Why doesn't somebody arrest them?"

"Who?" Britt asked. "What for? Maybe they haven't broken the law here."

"They tried to rob a train," she declared. "There's a United States marshal here. I saw his name in that newspaper you had."

"He'd be hard to find when you don't know what he looks like," Britt said thoughtfully. "Do you remember his name?"

"No. But what about the Army?"

"Both the Army and the Navy are reluctant to interfere in civilian affairs," Britt said. "This isn't a military reservation now. It's up to this town to get organized and enforce its own law."

"So what about us?"

"They didn't pay much attention to us, did they?"

Her face brightened with sudden discovery. "Oh, I know. It's because you aren't wearing your uniform. If you'd have been in uniform that Dink Casey would have known you and—"

"You don't think he remembers the loud-mouthed girl who kicked him down and got the police after him in St. Louis," Britt said.

Eve, suddenly mortified, clapped her hand over her mouth.

Britt said quietly, "The Casey gang is thinking about something besides us. They have something on their mind. We just weren't important to them." He smiled. "I don't think you need to worry about them."

"I wasn't," she said half angrily. "I was worrying about you. You haven't even got a gun."

"Dink Casey's pistol is somewhere in here." Britt punched the seabag. "But I expect I'd have been pretty well shot up before I could have found it. Why do you try to pick a fight with everyone you meet?"

"Maybe all of us Andrews are stinkers." Her smile was devilish, and tempting.

Britt said earnestly, "Well, please, declare a truce for a while. Just take life easy and avoid entanglements. I tramped over this townsite for hours looking for you. I'm tired."

A strange expression filled her eyes and she said, "You were looking for me?" It seemed to amaze her. "I'm sorry. I'll behave." She laid a hand on his arm. "We'll just sit here and rest—"

A new disturbance interrupted. This time brassy music, distance muffled, came sounding up the slope. Eve jumped to her feet.

The sound of cornet and drum grew louder. Britt got up wearily to look downhill in the direction of the music. He could see a capacious show tent erected there, a block up the slope above the freight depot.

The sidewall sections of the tent were being rolled up and as each section was raised the music became louder. A long yellow pennant floated gaily from the foretop peak center pole above the tent.

The pennant was lettered, its letters scrambling and unscrambling as the pennant doubled and snapped in the brisk wind. It took Britt a long minute to put the letters in order and read its message: *Stutz and Basil.*

With the sidewalls all lifted now the music of the brass band in the tent sallied forth bright and lively. On a stage beneath the edge of the tent a chorus of four girls in black tights and yellow fluted blouses danced vigorously.

The tent was less than a block away, and across the street from Britt and Eve's position. Details of the tent's shady interior were clearly visible.

Britt saw a wheel of fortune rigged on the tent's center pole. A slender man beside the wheel gave it a whirl and the clack of its celluloid tabs against the wheel's marking peg reached up the hill, rhythmic and audible.

A plank bar stretched along the south boundary of the tent.

Slanting rays of the afternoon sun glinted amberly on bottled whiskies arranged behind the bar. Gaming tables circled the tent's sawdust floor.

"I'll be damned," Eve exclaimed.

A thick-chested man in dark checkered vest, his yellow shirt voluminous and sleeve gartered, moved casually along the east border of the tent. He came outside, carrying a yellow malacca cane which he pointed at an angle skyward, and began a pitch-man's drone.

His carnival chant was hardly needed. Men were moving in toward the tent from all sides. Britt recognized the heavy, check-vested barker. He was the gambler Roody had introduced—Horst Stutz.

Eve grabbed Britt's arm, starting toward the tent.

He gave her a surprised glance.

She had anticipated him. "Don't be silly. It's all right. There are four girls on the stage, and I see another woman in there now."

Britt saw the other woman. She had come from a curtained boudoir behind the stage, moving with grace through the crowd of men. Her dress was a shoulder-strap affair, sedately worn, trimmed with ruffles and flounces, and Britt had seen her style in waterfront dives from Salem to Tripoli. Could Eve be so naive . . .

She was tugging impatiently at him.

He stalled. "You said we'd sit and rest."

She pointed impatiently. "There are tables and chairs—and they're in the shade. We can sit and rest there!"

Britt resisted the urge to anger. He knew that one wrong word could turn her impatience to anger and send her off full tilt for the gambling tent. He said firmly, "You promised young Decatur we'd hold his claim."

Eve surrendered. "Oh. Yes. I forgot."

She released Britt's arm and stood forlornly, watching the

excitement, her shoulders moving in rhythm with the brassy music.

The woman wearing the ruffles and flounces stepped out of the tent into the sunlight. Britt saw her eyes screw tight against the brightness. She quickly retreated into the shady tent, and walked on to pause beside the man at the wheel of fortune.

It confirmed Britt's guess; she was Inez Basil. The man at the wheel was George Basil, her husband.

The brass band finished a tune and immediately launched another. Boomers were three deep along the bar. George Basil was beginning to get some takers at his wheel.

"Quite a sight, isn't it?"

It was Joel Decatur, who had returned unnoticed from the river, carrying a bucket of water.

"Some splashed out." He was still breathing rapidly. "That's a long walk."

"Here, I'll drink the rest," Eve said thirstily.

From the duffel in his shelter tent Joel Decatur produced a tin cup. The level of water in the bucket lowered as Eve, Britt, and Joel drank.

The bucket was half emptied when Eve sat down on the ground. "You know," she sighed, "not being thirsty any more takes the starch out of me."

Joel eased down tiredly to sit on his heels. "I wonder what time it is?"

Britt calculated the declination of the sun, "It's almost six o'clock. The sun will set in less than an hour."

"I'd forgotten we had a navigator." Joel Decatur smiled.

"Let's eat," Eve suggested.

Joel prowled his duffel for a can opener.

"You came prepared," Britt commented.

Joel nodded as he cut open the container of dried beef Eve handed him. "A lawyer has to plan ahead."

Eve indicated the gambling tent. "How did they get that up so fast?"

Britt eyed her sidelong as Joel passed the container.

"The tent was standing when I arrived at the depot," Joel paused to bite a mouthful of the dried beef, "over an hour ago."

Recalling the men struggling up the hill with the roll of canvas, Britt guessed: "They managed to get it shipped in early."

Joel added a bite of hardtack to his chewing. "I think you'll find plenty of skulduggery has gone on. They probably also managed to have the lot staked in advance. I came in on the fourth train. There was nothing on this lot but a stake. Everyone was running past it. The law says it takes a human to hold a claim, not a wooden stick. I pulled up the stick and had started to set up my shelter tent when that pair came along—"

"How about some candy?" Eve offered the sack.

"Thank you." Joel dipped out a handful.

Activity stirred the long line of boomers extending now from the land office to the railroad tracks. They were moving methodically, each pausing at the land office doorway.

Joel Decatur nodded. "They're passing out numbered slips. We'll each get one. It will take days to register all these claims."

Britt drank another cup of the river water. The sun was a burning rim on the horizon. He studied Eve. "I've got to find a place for you to spend the night, young lady."

Eve crunched a piece of hard candy, and winked. "Like I said awhile ago, I'm with you."

Britt felt the heat of embarrassment rising again as he tried to recall: "There was something in the newspaper—a veteran named Evans—he and his wife were going to set up a boarding-house hotel—"

Joel pointed angling downhill. "About a block and a half northwest, down that way, some joined tents are going up. I think the sign said hotel."

Britt asked Eve, "Shall we go see?"

She did not move. "Are you going to stay there?"

"No, I'll return here and join Decatur in his shelter tent, if I'm welcome."

"You are," Joel agreed.

Eve's sigh seemed extravagantly soulful, "You're not worried about me, are you?"

"I'm thinking," Britt said measuredly, "that those conniving gents we interrupted here may decide to call on Decatur while he's asleep."

Joel said, "We could give her the shelter tent. We could sleep outside."

"In the foggy, foggy dew," Eve's eyes sparkled.

"Let's take a look at Logan Station's hotel accommodations first," Britt said firmly. He took her arm. Reluctantly Eve let herself be lifted to her feet.

There were four tents in the first group, joined each behind the other. A husky one-armed man bossed the crew now beginning to erect the second column. A third row of tents, spread flatly slack, lay on the ground.

"Mr. Evans?"

"At your service, sir." The one-armed Evans was square shouldered, barrel chested, his left arm as muscular as two normal arms.

"Are you open for business?" Britt asked.

"Since we staked down the first tent."

"This young lady needs lodging for the night. Will she be safe here?"

"Mother!" shouted Evans.

A gray-haired woman came from the first tent. Britt looked at her and felt assured. Evans was repeating Britt's request.

"We'll put her in the tent right behind ours," Mrs. Evans said. "Goodness knows we've plenty room. We thought we'd be overrun with lodgers the first night, but everyone seems to be holding down a claim."

Eve stood apathetically, taking no interest in the conversation.

Mrs. Evans apologized for not being ready to serve supper.

"I'm trying to get things arranged now in time so I can cook breakfast."

"I've eaten," Eve said dispiritedly. "Too much, I think. I feel dopey."

"Your day is catching up with you," Mrs. Evans said sympathetically.

Britt passed Eve's valise to the one-armed veteran, and left her with Mrs. Evans. He headed back toward Joel Decatur's camp.

The sun had set, the evening light turning a faded gray in which tents and moving figures gradually became flat, black silhouettes against the sky. Britt and Joel stood for a while on the edge of the town lot, observing the activity around them slacken with the onset of night.

As darkness settled the lamplit interior of the Stutz and Basil gambling tent glowed, a pink jewel of attraction. The night hush provided a damper, mellowing sounds of the newborn town. The brass band in the tent was affected, its music softened by the damp and cooling night air, making its repertoire sound more musical—*Put on Your Old Gray Bonnet, Golden Slippers, A Hot Time in the Old Town Tonight*. The music seemed to make Joel sentimental. He lamented his failure to thank Eve for providing so delightful a supper. "And you for standing by me," he told Britt. "I'd hate to be among the missing, come morning."

Britt, watching the bar operating briskly in the Stutz and Basil emporium, asked, "Is that place breaking the law?"

"I don't think so" was Decatur's opinion. "This town has not yet made any laws to be broken."

"I'd swear I read somewhere that whiskey selling would be illegal in Oklahoma," Britt said.

"A widely held misconception," Joel said. "It is not illegal to possess whiskey, or sell whiskey, *inside* Oklahoma Territory. But it is illegal to transport whiskey across the Indian Territory —which they had to do to get the whiskey here. I'm doubtful that Stutz or Basil would care to explain how they got it here.

There would be a question of *ex post facto* in charging them now—although the charge would literally seem to prove itself."

The brass band finished a spirited rendition with Stutz and Basil's four hurdy-gurdy girls dancing in spritely drill around the tiny stage. When the music ended, the camp noise of passing harness chink and steady nail-hammering became audible. Street talk, punctuated with an occasional shout, then a faraway gunshot, were part of the welter and racket of people preparing for the first night in the new town.

This undercurrent of evening sounds seemed dull and flat with the band silent, yet somehow suspenseful. The hurdy-gurdy girls disappeared inside their dressing tent. Brass band musicians, wearing red uniform coats, wandered out of the tent, taking a casual break. Britt watched a slight figure, carrying a guitar, appear from some far side and move slowly through the scattering of men who stood among the gambling tent's tables. It was Peardeedo.

Surely he's not going to risk what little money he has in that deadfall, Britt thought. He said to Joel, "I see a friend down there in the gambling tent. Let's walk over and meet him."

"I think I'll snooze awhile," Joel demurred. "Then you can sleep when things get quieter."

"You think you can sleep in this racket?"

"I'm tired enough," Joel admitted wearily.

By the time he reached the tent Peardeedo had climbed atop the piano in front of the stage and was already absorbed in the magic his fingers wrought in chords and arpeggios. Then Britt recalled—he's part of the entertainment. Peardeedo began singing a melancholy ballad as Britt passed under the periphery of the tent:

> *"Adios, muchachas*
> *Noviacitas, mis queridas—"*

Seeing Britt, Peardeedo smiled happily despite the mournful melody of his song. Britt answered with a friendly wink and

went on to the bar. He ordered beer. Horst Stutz, alone behind
the bar, drew the stein and served it with no sign of recognition.

Civilian clothes, thought Britt. I guess I'm camouflaged.

Willingly blending unidentified into the surroundings Britt
leaned his elbows on the planks to listen. The gambling tent
was doing plenty of business regardless of the busy activities
going on in the town outside.

The celluloid clicks of George Basil's wheel were louder than,
and out-of-rhythm with, Peardeedo's tune. Basil's eye-shaded
face was obtuse as he called numbers and confirmed bets.
A group of boomers assembled near Britt at the bar were grum-
bling sourly.

"—Sooners comin' out of every crack in the rocks," one boomer
groused bitterly.

"An' every creek bottom," another complainer added.

One aggressive bib-overall wearer leaned into the group to
charge in belligerent accusation: "They ain't the worst. The
worst are the ones that was already here—the govamint clerks,
the railroad agents—"

Peardeedo finished his ballad. The brass bandsmen began returning inside the tent, drifting up onto the stage. Britt angled
back through the tables and sat in an empty chair near the little
guitarist who was climbing down off the piano. Dominoes,
pitch, faro, poker, three-card monte, Britt noted there was con-
siderable choice of games of chance.

The strong pitch pine odor of the sawdust flooring the tent
mingled with smell of whiskey and sweaty men. The band settled in place and a brassy fanfare and drum roll brought Inez
Basil out on stage. She paused dramatically at the edge to nod
at the "professor" at the piano that she was ready.

Peardeedo whispered to Britt, "For her I am supposed to
warm the crowd to mood *emocionante*." He shrugged, "They
don't listen so well."

On stage, Inez Basil seemed to fit Roody's lyrical description
—"bittersweet." Her voice was husky. She knew her business.

Her song, of a young girl misled into a life of sin, was as sad as Peardeedo's, but performed with slick professionalism of gesture to make it suggestive, sultry, rather than urging virtue.

Britt said, "She does her work well," and half smiled at Peardeedo's answering eloquent shrug.

Britt gave Peardeedo an account of events since they had left the train at noon and finished his beer feeling that he had been gone overlong from Decatur's lot. While Inez Basil acknowledged the applause after her song Peardeedo tuned his guitar for another turn atop the piano and Britt left the tent.

As he walked uphill toward Joel's lot Logan Station's activity was holding steady. In the light of lanterns, studs of wooden buildings were rising, solid hammer raps nailing them in place. The noise of hammering and sawing came from everywhere.

Distantly then Britt heard women's voices. Not the sultry croon of Inez Basil, but many women's voices, singing raggedly, but in unison. They came from behind him, sounding vaguely religious, as if they might be coming from a camp meeting down near the depot.

Britt paused. The voices seemed nearer. He turned to look. The group was in the middle of the recently made street, marching through ruts of dust and patches of remaining grass. Their voices, high, reedy, and female, battled the discords of carpentry and town noise going on around them. The women carried pitch pine torches. As they came on the words that they sang became audible.

> "Onward, onward,
> On for temperance
> We must stri-i-i-ke a blow for right.
> Do not tarry,
> Do not falter
> Defeat booze this very night."

Torches high, flickering smokily in the darkness, the women approached the corner.

*"Onward, onward
On for temperance—"*

Britt watched them coming full on. They made their way past settlers, afoot and on horseback, who cluttered the street. It was the W.C.T.U. women, parading up from the depot, where it occurred to Britt their emigrant car may just have arrived. They split apart to pass a settler's laden wagon as it hauled slowly up the hill. The pulling horses shied and backed in the harness as the pine torches reflected in the team's blinder-shielded eyes.

The teamster's cursing overrode the women's song momentarily, the man yelling profanely at his team, then at "You damn fool women!"

"On for temperance"—the W.C.T.U. women sang loudly— "we must stri-i-ke a blow right right—"

They marched around the corner, Frances Chameau in the lead carrying a cloth banner emblazoned with one word, TEMPERANCE. The torch-bearing formation behind her, now Britt saw Annette among them, straggled loosely, their long skirts brushing the street where grassy prairie earth sliced with wagon ruts and churned by hoofs and trampling feet made thin dust.

"Do not tarry—" they sang in rash boldness as if trying to dispel their own forebodings.

"—do not falter—" The pine torches flickered wind blown and fitful. The women tried to straighten their disorganized and unmilitary ranks, then striking out once more with determined stride, torches flaring "—defeat booze this very night!"

Britt spoke aloud in sudden alarm, "Confound! They're headed for the gambling tent."

10

Britt ran to the corner.

Hurrying along the edge of the street, he followed as the crusading delegation marched on toward the big Stutz and Basil tent.

Men at the gambling tables had begun to stand as the singing W.C.T.U. women reached the tent edge. Then uncertainty began to plague both sides. The banner carried by Mrs. Chameau became entangled in the tent's ropes. A striped-suited gentleman moved from a table to help untangle it. Then he read its legend, and at the same time seemed to comprehend the words being sung. He stepped aside in hesitant confusion.

Mrs. Chameau jerked vigorously at the banner and it wrenched loose. She led the way on into the tent. The arrangement of tables inside separated the women, breaking their solid phalanx front. The temperance women wandered among the tables as their ranks split apart.

They kept on singing, but not overconfidently, straggling far apart like rivulets oozing across dry earth. They halted then, and at once began moving together for comfort and support, tightening their ranks. The brass band was not on stage.

Peardeedo had apparently just climbed back atop the piano. The women's singing seemed to overcome him with awe. The gambling games were suspended. One man gripped his cards against his chest like a woman concealing herself in modesty. At the pitch table a player's hand poised dangling in air. In astonishment he still held the card he had been about to play.

Among the men Britt saw expressions of surprise, cynical

amusement, irritation, scorn. Horst Stutz came rushing from behind the bar in anger.

He was staring in appalled fury at the pitch-pine torches and he rushed bull-like to grab the torch of the first woman he reached. "Damn it and hell!" His shout had a heavy German accent. "You crazy woman! You trying to set the place on fire?"

Stutz threw the torch in the sawdust, stomping it in fury and panic to kill its flames.

"Sir!" Frances Chameau raised her arm to bring the imperfect singing to an end. "You who sell this demoniac whiskey"—her voice was trembling—"brewed by the very fires of perdition. You fear our torches? Your whiskey burns men's souls! You send them bound for the raging fires of hell! Our small temporal flames—"

Stutz shoved her rudely out of the way reaching for another torch, as his partner George Basil came from the wheel.

"Stop!" Basil grabbed Stutz's thick arm. His partner's cold order interrupted Horst Stutz's blundering panic, and Basil spoke coldly to Mrs. Chameau: "Madam, if you don't mind, we'll await our time for perdition. This place is a tinder box—the tent —the sawdust—"

Stutz broke away from his partner then and ran toward a group of the band musicians at the bar. "Play! Play!" he yelled in Teutonic rage.

The W.C.T.U. contingent launched raggedly into their own marching song: "Onward, onward—on for temperance—"

Stutz swerved about herding the musicians. He hurried them across the tent toward the platform and their instruments. With discord and raggedness equal to the women's singing the band finally began playing *A Hot Time in the Old Town Tonight*.

To the musical conflict now were added shouts of male hilarity. The brass band was winning the unequal contest, drowning out the ladies' singing. Disorder began to stir among the crowd of men in the tent. Some of the drinkers had been at the bar since the first raising of the tent's sidewalls.

The boozy boomer Britt had heard griping about "Sooners"

to justify his own failure to stake a claim staggered toward Annette Chameau. As the band's brazzy noise ended, the women still sang, having wandered off tune, but rallying as the band ceased.

Another drunken barfly, his eyes aglint with incendiary ideas, suggested loudly, "Stick yer torch up agin' that canvas, honey. Ol' Stutz'll have a hot time!" He shoved off the bar and reeled toward a thin-armed, torchbearing woman whose lank face had assumed the dead-white pallor of terror.

The disappointed boomer reached Annette. He swayed boozily as he put a hairy arm around her waist.

"Hey," he yowled. "Here's one'll give *me* a hot time!"

Britt arrived to peel the boomer's arm from Annette's waist and shove the man away. The boomer fell and slid, forcefully, plowing sawdust with his shoulders. He was struggling to arise when Britt stepped on his wrist.

The firebug's urgent suggestion had brought no action so he reached to confiscate the thin woman's torch. Horst Stutz came running to wrap fat arms around him from behind. They fell, wrestling. George Basil, cool and hard, stamped out the fallen torch in the sawdust, then backed slowly, ferreting the crowd with vigilance. Except for the grunting of Stutz, wrestling with the boomer incendiary, and a squeal of pain from the man who now gripped Britt's leg in desperate struggling to remove Britt's boot from his wrist, a silent lull imminent with threat fell over the crowd of men in the tent.

Into this ominous hush, Peardeedo, from atop the piano, spoke with careless ease. With offhandedness as gentle as a yawn, he asked in the menacing silence, "How about this verse, *muchachos?*"

His brown fingers plucked a lazy arpeggio, and he sang an improvised parody of the W.C.T.U. marching song:

> *"Onward, onward*
> *To the bar, boys.*
> *Es time to dreenk—not time to fight—"*

The emotionally charged heat in the tent seemed to congeal for an instant as men on the edge of violence paused. In that chilly instant, to Britt's eyes, the poised men seemed to become a tentful of waxen statues.

Peardeedo's voice was soft, gentle, and soothing, but his dark eyes found George Basil in hard-searching gaze:

> *"Breeng on the girls, boss*
> *Their petticoats toss*
> *Es such a hap-py dizzy sight."*

Britt could almost smell the scorch of cordite. The atmosphere in the tent was as acrid as a fuse sputtering toward the touch hole of a cannon. Britt glanced at Peardeedo, wondering how long the little Mexican could stave off the riot he was postponing.

Peardeedo's face was smooth and placid but there was urgency in his eyes and in the stare which he locked on George Basil.

The guitar strings vibrated with hypnotic tempo under his slender fingers, and Peardeedo sang a little louder:

> *"The dancing girls weel*
> *Kick and squeal—we'll feel*
> *Not so bad and mad—"*

The little minstrel quit playing then, suddenly, and spoke out loud, "Ain't that right?"

The desperation in Peardeedo's question finally untracked George Basil. He moved in smoothly to the dressing cubicle and lifted its flap. Basil's spoken order primed the musicians.

The brass band leader fumbled clumsily through his music, calling, *"Orpheus*, boys!"

The cornets blared into the opening strains of Offenbach's Can-can and the hurdy-gurdy girls came tumbling out on the stage threshing their skirts.

Britt lifted his foot from the wrist of the boomer. The man

massaged his wrist, grimacing, his lusty ardor distracted by the pain. Britt looked around the tent. Its occupants, scraggly whiskered, skinny red-necks, jaundiced, dyspeptic, pallid gamblers, sodbusters, leather-vested cowboys in fringed shotgun chaps, suit-wearing townsmen, all seemed to be staring in happy digression at the hurdy-gurdy girls.

So Britt lifted his arms and, like shooing a flock of hens out of a chicken coop, shooed the W.C.T.U. women out of the tent. Horst Stutz and the firebug were still wrestling seatily on the sawdust, ignored by the men around them who craned to watch the leggy Can-can on stage.

Britt's little clutch of chastened crusaders drew small attention as he shooed them out. The girls on stage, voluptuous with hourglass convexity of bust and hips, their shapely legs gyrating from a froth of red and black ruffles, had drawn all interest away from Britt's female charges. It was a cowering and badly frightened group of women that Britt finally rounded to a halt at the corner a half block north of the Stutz and Basil tent.

They had extinguished their torches and stood holding the sooty pine brands low, away from their clothing. Smoke, odorous and smudgy, curled from dead torch ends. Britt faced them and was about to speak when he was kissed. It was Annette. Her lips were soft, sweet, and cool. The kiss lingered.

Britt stood wide-eyed in surprise that grew to utter astonishment, staring at Annette's eyelids. Her eyes were closed, her lashes trembling. The sweetness of her kiss overcame all other sensations and he simply stood, tasting the cool flavor of Annette Chameau's lips.

Wisps of her hair blown fragrantly against his face by the evening wind began to rouse a stronger sensation in him. Annette made no indication that the kiss would end. Britt's arms were at half-mast, held at the exact point to which he had raised them as he had commenced to call the ladies to attention. Mrs. Chameau stepped to pluck her daughter's sleeve.

Annette paused to glance curiously at her mother, and began raising her face again toward Britt.

Mrs. Chameau said sharply, "Annette!"

The girl gave her mother a mild look.

Mrs. Chameau said, "Lieutenant Pierce has saved us all and perhaps you should let each of us thank him in our own way. Rather than trying alone to discharge the entire debt yourself."

Annette did not seem abashed. She simply stepped away, mildly unashamed.

Britt completed raising his arms. "Ladies—" He found that he had forgotten what he intended to say. Trying to recover from his own confusion, Britt noted that the shock which had stunned these women seemed to be lifting. They faced toward him and he felt a sense of having their attention. They were waiting for direction.

"Do you have a place to stay for the night?" he asked.

There was a murmur of voices saying no.

Mrs. Chameau began: "The railroad uncoupled our car and left us on the Arkansas City siding until the very last train—"

A few of the smudging torches, fanned by the night wind, were popping aflame again. Britt interrupted: "Let me suggest that those of you who still have torches throw them into the street."

Some of them had done so after leaving the Stutz and Basil tent. A scattering of the flickering, smoldering pine brands traced the way back to the gambling tent, but some of the women seemed to have forgotten they held them. "There's danger you may catch each other's clothing on fire, or burn your hands," Britt finished.

The smudging brands made a flaring bonfire as the pile of them grew at the edge of the street. In its flickering light Mrs. Chameau continued: "Mrs. Porter"—she indicated a gaunt and sickly woman—"became ill on the way down. Our charter on the car expired on reaching Logan Station. The railroad has pulled it away. We remained in the depot caring for Mrs. Porter until she felt able to march—"

Britt could not resist the temptation. "I won't disparage your cause," he broke in, "but you ladies nearly bred a disaster."

"We have been chastened by this failure," Mrs. Chameau said sharply. "We would like to thank you, Lieutenant—" Her head was high and her voice was fast attaining its former ring. The firelight gave spark to her eyes and, grimly, Britt interrupted again.

"May I lead your group to shelter?" he asked.

Mrs. Chameau continued sternly, "We would like to thank you, Lieutenant—"

Damn, Britt thought. "You owe me no thanks," he contradicted. "Your thanks should go to a mighty quick-witted little Mexican *cancionero* who saved all of you from one hell of a mauling. Now follow me!"

His tone brooked no discussion. The women came.

As he led them down the street he said in explanation to Annette who walked beside him, "You recall Eve Andrews? You met her this morning as we got off the train in Arkansas City. I found a tent hotel room for Miss Andrews earlier this evening—" The chill rising beside him drew his attention.

Annette was walking briskly, tight-lipped, and staring ahead. Britt's impulse to explain cooled. The antipathy these two girls seemed to have for each other struck him as odd, especially considering that they had barely spoken.

Strange, he thought. Britt dismissed it from mind and they walked on toward the Evans' hotel in strained silence. As he led the coterie of thirty females onto the lot where a dozen tents now stood ready it created a new stir of amazement.

The one-armed veteran and his wife heard Britt's explanation through, and Mrs. Evans bustled into action.

"We are surely pleased to have you ladies," she declared. "We'd thought we would be full, but everyone is holding down a claim. We surely appreciate you bringing us all this custom, Lieutenant. Mr. Evans will have to set up more cots—"

Evans went about his work. Britt inquired about Eve.

"I'm sure she's sound asleep." Mrs. Evans parted the entrance flaps to admit the ladies to the largest of the tents. "She was all fagged out." Her harried gaze swept the file of women as she followed them inside. "You *all* look fagged out." She began unstacking folded canvas chairs, "This is going to be our dining room before morning, we hope. Won't you all take a chair and sit?"

Britt remained in the entryway to announce, "Ladies, I'll bid you good night."

Mrs. Chameau was busily telling Mrs. Evans something about ". . . my recommendation for our next assault on that iniquitous place. I intend to press it strongly . . ." Britt felt Annette's cool gaze on him, her composure unruffled. Vaguely, he offered a smile and backed out of the tent.

Britt walked uphill at a deliberate gait toward Joel Decatur's claim. Exhaustion had taken its toll of him, and of Logan Station. Languor slowed his pace to an indolent stroll. *It gets steeper every time I climb it,* he thought.

The general noise had decreased, sounding night-muffled and inert. Work was in progress on some of the lots, but the workers moved slow and laggardly. A few men, stumbling about, numb with fatigue, worked doggedly as if unable to give up.

They'll work until they drop from exhaustion, and sleep where they fall, Britt thought. He paused on reaching Joel's lot to stand and look out over the newborn town.

Out in the darkness, as far as he could see, campfires burned. Thousands of campfires, under the dark cover of night. The flickering small blazes reached across the hills, trifling flimsy sparks. Feebly burning, but not one entirely losing its battle with the darkness.

Britt unbuttoned his collar. *Some watch I've stood,* he thought.

11

Britt squatted uncomfortably to loosen boot laces, then crawled fully dressed into the shelter tent to awaken the sleeping Joel. Decatur responded, and crawled out of the tent. Britt slid groggily into the bed roll Joel left. The camp grew more quiet, even as he dozed off to sleep. He awoke an hour later to a lethargic silence broken by insect noises, a steady metallic racket. Then Britt heard the plodding rhythm of yoked oxen and a dull resonant clank of the bell on a lead ox.

A caravan was approaching the camp. Britt turned, shifting his position on the lumpy ground, and went back to sleep. Joel woke him at 4 A.M.

Britt relieved the watch and stood in darkness before the shelter tent, stretching life into muscles stiffened by the spring damp earth. He felt alert, somewhat rested, much better. The thousand fires out across the dark hills had burned to embers.

The glowing embers gave faint shape to the low, sprawling roll of the hills. Britt scanned their contours, the horizon around, and leaned to heave out the seabag which bulged the sloping tent end at Joel's feet. Joel, breathing in deep regularity, did not stir.

Britt loosed the knotted lanyard and sorted down through the seabag's contents. The hard lump of Dink Casey's Colt passed his palm. Britt's fingers found wool and, carefully, to avoid disturbing the fold of the packed garments, he extracted his uniform and fresh underwear.

Shaking out the uniform, Britt used the privacy of night to change from the rough clothing in which he had slept. By the

time he had laid out the sweat-smelly drawers and butternut
garments he had worn, weighting them with chunks of sandstone to air and later sun, the east horizon was gray.

Britt walked the circumference of the claim lot. The early
morning was damply chill, the fading night turning a lighter
gray, and a dog's lonely, distant bark was answered by a baying
yawp down toward the river.

Dog conversation followed, joined by sporadic dog comments
from every direction. In the crescendo of woofing yawp and
bark, Britt decided there must be almost as many dogs as there
were camps.

A nearby hound's bay quavered to rising howl and all the
canine talk became discordant song. As the numberless camp
dogs howled in unison the massive lamentation of eerie, lonesome sound halted Britt. He stood, hackling, at the many toned
wail. The grief and sorrow of souls mourning in torment seemed
in it.

It sounded wild and timeless, like nothing he had ever
heard before, and bespoke a kinship reaching back toward man's
own ancient wildness. It held on primitive and tremoring, and
into it men's shouts flung hoarse command for quiet.

The curses and coarse shouts brought an ebb in the weird din.
It ended as comfortless as it had begun, and in the silence that
followed rose the sporadic clink of metal and undertones of
roused activity. On nearby claims the desultory pot and pan
sounds of readying breakfast commenced, scattered, haphazard,
random, and continuous. Logan Station was awakening.

Forms now visible in the gray dawn moved to stir fires and
the clonk of axe on wood, cutting and splitting chunks to quicken
their burning became intermittent. Britt heard the unmistakable
chink of an iron coffeepot lid. In the low bottoms, where the
river bent around the depot, mist hung.

A foggy drab, bleached white in the increasing light, obscured the boles of the dark-leafed trees, the thick grove curving

along the river's bend, turning southwest beyond the depot, and disappearing on its southwesterly course.

Britt looked aloft at the sky. It was entirely clear, a veil of domed pink gauze. Eastward and down from the zenith it turned to gaudy hues fast becoming transparent at the horizon. The sun was rising.

He swung his gaze to observe a figure angling upward in a long jaywalk from the direction of the Evans tents. It was Eve.

She came on the lot looking sleepy. "Shucks. I'd hoped to catch you asleep," she said.

Britt nodded toward the shelter tent where Joel slept. "Decatur's still asleep," he suggested. "Rouse him out."

Eve raised the tent flap and looked down at Joel's heavy brogans. She dropped the tent flap then and scrutinized Britt. "You certainly are duded up this morning. A sea-going Yankee bluebelly ready to stand inspection."

"That outfit was getting overripe." He nodded at the clothes he had laid out to air.

"Stinky, huh?" Eve said. "I had a spit bath last night."

Britt involuntarily found himself visualizing the image of Eve standing naked before a basin, washing herself. Still involuntarily, he said tersely, "Damn!"

"What's bit you now?" she asked innocently.

He had driven the image away, but he still felt like a Peeping Tom caught peering through her tent fly.

Eve broke in on his recrimination to ask, "Are you carrying that gun—the one you took away from Dink Casey?"

"No."

She asked, "Are you sending formal invitations to your killing?"

"What are you talking about?"

"It's either that, or you plan to get shot and die secretly," Eve said callously. "The Caseys saw us yesterday. I've been thinking about what you said. I think you're wrong. I don't think they've got anything else on their minds. I think the first time Dink

Casey sees you where it's nice and quiet he'll kill you. Maybe me too."

Britt gave it some thought. "Carrying sidearms usually causes more trouble than it cures," he shrugged.

"Have it your way." Her answer did not sound like agreement. "Maybe the Caseys are far, far away, robbing the rich to give to the poor."

She left the subject. "Mrs. Evans says she'll have breakfast ready at sunup."

Britt squinted eastward. The sun had cracked the horizon like the heel of a red-hot horseshoe above smoldering coals in a blacksmith's forge.

"That's now," he said.

"Let's go," Eve suggested.

Britt's and Eve's conversation had roused Joel Decatur from slumber. He lay contemplating the sun-bright golden brown of the canvas above him, listening sleepily to the talk of the pair outside his tent, then sat up and scooted forward.

He emerged from the shelter tent to sit round-shouldered and slumping over the loose strings of his half-laced brogans, blinking drowsily as he watched Britt and Eve descend the slope toward the Evans tents.

With their approach to the boardinghouse tent came the tangle of female chatter. Britt opened the entrance flap. The W.C.T.U. women were up, dressed and assembled around the long plank tables, rising sporadically by twos and threes to assist Mrs. Evans at the stove or in serving the tables, and chattering constantly.

Britt was seated and served with deference. The middle-aged ladies, astonishingly coy now in his presence, made him aware of the stature he had assumed.

Eve ate her breakfast, increasingly curious at all the attention

Britt was receiving and finally asked, "What is this, your harem?"

Britt gave her a sketchy account of the W.C.T.U.'s assault on the gambling tent.

"Peardeedo sounds like the hero," Eve commented. "Why do *you* rate such devotion?"

She poked at the egg on her plate. "All that excitement happened after you left me here last night?"

Britt nodded, carving his ham.

She sounded regretful: "And I slept through it all!"

Annette, breakfasting beside her mother, had given Britt a nod of cool composure. Her demeanor was strangely detached, and Britt recalled a time when he was six years old, and in a riverfront general store had begged his mother for a brightly illustrated red-backed book.

His mother had explained that he was too young to read the book, putting him off by suggesting that perhaps when he grew older—Britt recalled that he had lost interest in the book then, and he wondered now what had called that memory to mind.

Eve whispered, "Let's get out of this biddy house."

They stood at the grassy edge where the turf had been cut by the steady passing of wheels and hoofs until it had become, in reality, a street. A block to their right stood the silent gambling tent, its side walls dropped and mute.

A flatbed hayrack on which low benches had been nailed approached, coming uphill. A scattering of passengers rode the benches. Its drover was shouting, "Omnibus wagon. Anywhere in town for two bits."

The heavy team pulled close aboard, passing with strong horsey odor. Britt called to the driver. A deep-throated "whoa" brought the wagon to a halt a yard beyond them. The driver caught the half dollar Britt spun toward him and Eve was already seated as Britt vaulted aboard beside her.

As the wagon pulled around the corner and up the main street Nate Richter jumped aboard.

He came stepping across the seats, balancing himself against the wagon's movement, his face a tight, dark frown.

"Trouble?" Eve asked as Richter sat down facing them.

"Too much work to do," Richter said.

"And you're taking time off to go for a ride?" Eve asked.

"Up to the land office. We worked all night getting the press set up. Hope to get out an afternoon paper. My printer and his devil are setting handbills now. I've got to cover a town meeting at the depot."

Richter glanced over his shoulder at the approaching land office and stood up.

"Going to register your claim?" Eve asked.

"It will be a week before my number comes up," Richter scowled. "I'm hunting news for our first edition."

Britt glanced down the busy street. "Looks like you ought to sell plenty papers."

"More people came through Ark City on their way here than passed through there during the California gold rush." Richter swung off the side of the wagon, waving as he disappeared into the land office.

The wagon rolled on downhill. Britt inhaled deeply. It was like a fine morning at sea. The sun stood some sixty degrees above the horizon, its azimuth northerly. Already warm, it would be hot at this latitude when the sun reached its zenith. *Long days, and bright sunshine,* Britt thought.

A six-span yoke of oxen was drawn up before the 2 x 4 studs of a store under construction. Two sweating freighters were unloading a cookstove from the freight wagonload of hardware to which the oxen were yoked. The frantic haste that had characterized yesterday was gone. Logan Station was pacing itself, working purposefully, without wasted effort.

All down the street construction was in progress, the slope of the hill a forest of upraised studs above floor sections of fresh yellow pine. The sharp fragrance of cut lumber filled the morning air. Sheathing, clapboards, car siding, had begun to ascend outside walls. The steady clat of hammers, the rasp of crosscut and ripsaw, accompanied the unloading of merchandise to be set down among the carpenters erecting the buildings.

At the foot of the street where the land leveled, the government chain crew had laid out new blocks since yesterday. In the distance, the miniature figure of a transit man was visible, signaling to his stake man. The clear atmosphere tapered off into blue ozone above acres of tents. Walking men, horsemen, buggies, wagons, and the sun's sharp glinting on harness buckles, wagon tire rims, bright metallic objects, made constant movement.

Eve called out, "Zack! Zack Hall!"

The grizzled rancher was leaning on a gin-pole set in new earth, watching a foundation crew dig footings. He turned, squinting into the sun to discover Britt and Eve in the passing wagon and yelled at the driver.

The wagon team pulled up and Hall came stiffly to climb up over a wagon spoke. He needed a shave, his face gray-stubbled and tired, but he began talking as he lowered himself onto the bench where Richter had sat. "Feller there"—Zack nodded toward the excavation—"says he's going to have the first brick building in town. Where you all headed?"

The wagon rolled with a rough lurch over deep-cut sod ruts.

"Up toward the land office," Britt reported.

"I been hanging around town," Zack said soberly, "to help my boys record claims when they come in."

Eve asked, "How did your cowboys make out in the race?"

The elderly rancher sat watching the uneven rocking of the wagon's flat bed. "I'd of lost my bet," he told her.

The wagon rounded the corner, turning south.

"We didn't get a third of the sections we aimed for," Hall said. "I'm going to have to cut my operations mighty close. There ain't no doubt. The grangers are takin' over."

Hall's face was grave. They traversed the block, turning up-hill. Britt considered how it must be for a man like Hall, seeing his way of life changed by events beyond his control. The un-focus of Hall's eyes, lost in remembering, reminded Britt of sad-ness he had seen in the faces of officers telling of hard days in the Navy following the Civil War.

Of tenure in rank without promotion, of ships built of green timber that disintegrated in heavy seas. Most lately, the Navy's Samoan disaster. Poor planning. Here a headlong rush of settlers to turn grassland under the plow. *Hurry up,* Britt thought, *and do it wrong.* The wagon crested the rise and the horses eased in the harness, drawing the wagon along level land.

Hall was pensive. "I been thinkin' about maybe puttin' to-gether a show," he said. "Lieutenant, do you reckon Eastern dudes would pay to watch a man ride a buckin' horse? Or see a steer throwed and tied?"

Eve wiggled on the seat. "I saw Buffalo Bill Cody in a play in St. Louis," she said. "The play was terrible but the theater was crowded."

Britt grinned. "There's your answer."

"I don't mean no play actin' thing," Zack insisted. "I mean real cowboys ridin' rough string horses. Indians in paint an' feathers—"

"You'd have to have some play acting," Eve argued. "Have a stagecoach holdup, like the one that happened over on the Cimarron last week! Have your Indians attack the stagecoach. Cowboys to the rescue—"

Zack studied her. "You remind me of a coffeepot percolating. What do you think, Pierce? Would people pay to see that kind of show?"

"Seafaring is my business," Britt smiled. "Not dramatics. A quarterdeck watch deals in realities."

Hall declared ruefully, "Cow work was real enough—used to be."

The omnibus wagon rode up against the singletrees, the

team holding back its weight as the downgrade steepened. The strain slackened as the wagon turned the corner facing the Stutz and Basil tent. The freight depot lay just downhill, and seeing it Britt said, "I'm going to drop off here. I've got a sea chest in that pile of freight down there. Maybe I'd better sight it before time to disembark tomorrow." Rising, he told Eve, "I'll see you later at the Evans," and swung down off the wagon bed.

"No, you won't," Eve yelled. "I'm coming with you."

She leaped and fell against him, breathing hard from the sudden exertion. A sudden excitement flooded Britt Pierce, then he released her, somewhat confused. As they stepped apart to walk down to the freight depot they walked sedately, side by side.

The steepness of the hill made walking difficult and they held back, each step a jolting resistance against the cindered embankment of the tracks, then they walked the railroad ties toward the hustling confusion of the freight depot.

Lumber that had been stacked neatly beside the right of way during the train's arrival yesterday had become a tangled and depleted stock. A harried dealer, making change from the pockets of a carpenter's apron, sold the lumber on a serveyourself basis to impatient buyers who worked among the helterskelter stacks.

The litter of boards, crisscrossed as though heaped by a haphazard wind, remained to be climbed over and tugged at, by men hurrying to load anything close to the dimension they sought on wagons angled and backed crookedly up to the right of way.

"That's handy," Eve said. "Why move your stock? Sell it at the depot."

On down the freight platform sweating seekers dug through crates and boxes on the dock.

Britt shook his head in dismay.

Eve's eyes, exploring the crowd, lit on a railroad employee in black sleeve guards. He was walking backward, restraining the momentum of a handcart laden with battered packages. A clutter of freight tickets were thrust in the band of his cap. Eve walked down the ramp to tap him on the shoulder.

"You work here?" she asked.

"Work here?" The man's eyes rolled. "My god, I'm the freight agent."

"We're looking for a sea chest," Eve said.

The freight agent looked at Britt's pillbox cap. "Are you a conductor for another line?"

Britt shook his head. "U. S. Navy."

With lethargic grunt the agent instructed, "Let me see your baggage check."

Britt took it from his wallet.

The freight agent studied it, and said, "This is for Los Angeles."

"The conductor changed my ticket to Logan Station."

"Well, he didn't change your baggage check. Here sailor"—the agent shoved the wrinkled pasteboard back into Britt's hand.

"So where's my sea chest?" Britt asked.

"Halfway to California." The agent lifted his cart, dumped it empty, and dragged it back up the ramp into the depot.

"That's interesting." Britt snapped the cardboard thoughtfully, and pocketed it.

"Where shall we go now?" Eve asked.

"Where do you want to go?"

"Right over there," she pointed.

The cherubic face of Reverend Obadiah Quigley was the target at which she pointed. With untroubled disregard for the confusion around him, the youthful Reverend was making his way across the opposite end of the platform toward the passenger entrance of the depot.

They caught him as he reached the door.

"Leaving?" Eve challenged.

"No, no," he said pleasantly. "I'm expecting Mrs. Quigley. She really should have arrived. I thought the telegrapher might have a wire."

Eve was ironic. "If he has, it will be crossed."

"Patience." Reverend Quigley smiled genially.

"This place is working," she declared, "like yeast in a crock of home brew."

The congenial Quigley remained unshaken. "It reminds me of the sorcerer's apprentice."

Eve recalled: "The broom wouldn't quit bringing water. The trains won't quit bringing people."

Britt nodded. "It's time for the sorcerer to appear."

"Not until the train brings my wife," the preacher urged.

Britt surveyed the frantic depot activity. "Each train brings more people, and more disorder."

Quigley's agreement was again tempered. "Patience. Rome wasn't built in a day."

Eve observed, "Logan Station is, as sure as the devil—sorry, parson."

Quigley nodded. "I'm sure he's here, too."

Eve frowned. "We saw four of his disciples yesterday. The Casey gang."

Quigley agreed. "Sinister men. However"—his countenance inevitably brightened—"there are righteous disciples here also."

"The W.C.T.U.?" Eve said glumly.

Not understanding, Quigley said, "I beg your pardon?"

Britt recounted the women's attempt to raid the Stutz and Basil gambling tent.

Reverend Quigley heard the account through. "Where are the good ladies now?"

Eve pointed uphill, describing the location of the Evans tents.

"I must call on them. I'll check to see if there's a wire from Mrs. Quigley." The reverend pushed back into the depot.

"I suppose he'll lead the next assault on Stutz and Basil," Britt speculated.

"He'll get hurt," Eve said flatly.

"Don't underrate the preacher," Britt said. "I've seen fat men who could absorb punishment like a sponge."

They walked on uphill toward the center of town.

"There's the print shop." Eve stopped. Richter was visible through the doorway of the small new clapboard office.

Eve yelled across the street, "Mister Editor, where is the Commercial Bank in this town?"

"The banner just went up," Richter yelled in answer. "It's on the corner east of the land office."

Eve waved.

Richter called after her, "Here's a late news bulletin. Citizens are having a meeting at the depot this afternoon to elect town officers."

"He'll scoop his own newspaper," Eve said. They crossed to climb the second uphill block. Through the interlace of wagons and men jamming the land office intersection Britt saw Joel Decatur. Joel had rigged a line across his lot and was hanging wet garments on it as he wrung them out from a wash bucket between his feet.

Eve preceded Britt in entering the tiny frame bank. They stepped aside to avoid the steady in and out flow of customers. Roody was busy.

Behind a chest-high counter Roody was at work, his flushed face visible over a litter of deposit forms, ledgers, and counter cheques. He recognized Eve and glared at her.

Behind the counter stood a Mosler safe, its circular door swung open to reveal neat piles of money, bank drafts, and a small horde of jewelry and valuables customers had left for safekeeping.

A customer departed with a deposit slip and Roody shoved open the counter gate motioning Britt and Eve to enter. Shelved beneath the counter Britt saw the blue metal of a new 10-gauge shotgun, its glossy walnut stock an inch from Roody's knee. Britt followed Eve on into the back room.

In this small room of unpainted wall planks a camp cot with rumpled bedding was crowded against the west wall. An ancient dark varnished rolltop desk filled the center of the room. Strewn with papers, the desk seemed monstrous.

Eve inspected the room and returned to lean in the doorway. "Attention, little brother," she said blandly.

Roody spun.

"I'm busy," he spat. He turned to smile at his customer, a tough-faced boomer who was intent on stripping a money belt from around his waist. Roody turned back to Eve.

"My cashier hasn't arrived," he said angrily. "I can't hire any help." He glanced back at the customer who was working diligently on the last buckle of the money belt.

"I got up the hill too late to stake a claim. Had to buy this lot at an exorbitant price." Roody's attention flicked back and forth between Eve and the boomer.

"The men I hired as carpenters were bunglers—" The boomer's money belt swung loose and he flapped it on the counter as Roody finished, "—and they quit before the building was done."

The boomer said, "There's five thousand dollars in that money belt."

"I worked most of last night getting this building ready to open." Roody began extracting money from the belt.

The boomer was rubbing his middle with relief. "Carried that thing all the way from Chicago."

Roody sorted the money into piles. "These overloaded trains have bollixed everything. I don't know *where* my cashier is. I checked the schedule of transfers before I left Kansas City but no funds have arrived. I'm doubtful it's safe to ship money east." He said to the boomer, "Five thousand dollars, you say?"

The boomer nodded.

Roody asked Eve: "Where have you been lallygagging around?"

The boomer interrupted: "Are you transacting business or fighting with your wife?"

"My wife!" The thought seemed to stun Roody. He laughed sarcastically, "You have a wry wit, sir."

Roody finished counting. "Five thousand. Correct, sir."

The boomer's lips worked silently as he laboriously read the deposit receipt Roody had written and shoved across the counter, then he turned and left the bank.

Roody put the money belt in the safe.

"How may I serve you, madam," Roody asked pleasantly. His congeniality with this customer, contrasted with the snarling complaints he had been hurling at Eve, stirred Britt's amusement.

Like a burlesque comedian performing with two hats, Roody overplayed both parts. The fat lady asked to see the statement of Roody's parent bank. Roody supplied it with charismatic smile. The fat lady simpered.

Eve, leaning lethargically in the doorway, said, "Banker Andrews and his puppet show."

Britt put his shoulders against the wall and grinned, feeling a sheepish embarrassment for both of them.

Eve straightened, listening with attentive curiosity to some noise outside.

Britt, turning his attention from Eve, saw Roody's customers hurriedly leaving the bank. Roody watched the exodus in confusion and Eve stepped through the doorway. An urgent need to see what was transpiring seemed to grip Roody and he pushed past his sister. Britt followed them out into the street.

From this vantage point of the hillcrest Britt saw the crowd being drawn downhill toward Joel Decatur's lot. The crowd farther down the street was forming a ring. Joel's lot was the arena.

There were four men in the arena, Joel, Quentin Nash, Matt Lang, and a fourth man Britt did not recognize. The fourth man was jerking down Joel's clothesline. He was a domineering well-dressed man, and he strode now to throw the line of wet clothes into the street.

Joel's wet laundry splashed dust as it hit the street. The man tramped back on the lot to heave at the stake ropes of Joel's shelter tent. Britt began shouldering his way downhill.

12

Britt could hear Eve's short breathing as she ran up behind him. He felt her fingers then, catching the back of his uniform jacket, and he crowded on, making steady progress through the welter of humanity and towing Eve in his wake.

With the advantage of height Britt watched Joel's lot over the heads and shoulders of the jammed crowd before him. The burly, irate man, holding a tent rope he had uprooted, was delivering Joel a lecture.

Joel stood with crossed arms, his demeanor one of moderate equanimity although wary. Britt, plowing through the crowd, was still yards away when Joel's antagonist finished his lecture, threw down the tent rope he was holding and turned away.

Beckoning his henchmen, parting the crowd with broad gestures, the burly man led Nash and Lang across the street and into the land office. Joel's tent, sagging from the uprooted rope, remained half standing.

With the excitement over, the crowd lessened and Britt's going became easier.

Eve puffed breathlessly behind him, "Hey!" She came up alongside. "What's the excitement?"

Britt, shaking his head, took her arm.

The crowd drifted off. Bunches of idlers remained to gossip around the lot. Joel saw Britt and Eve approaching. He smiled and came into the street to meet them and retrieve his wet, dirty clothing.

Britt said, "What was that about?"

"Just more harassment." Joel patiently removed clothespins

from garments doughy with mud and dust. He walked back on the lot and dropped them in the bucket of water.

Methodically, he went to work on the loose tent rope. Britt pitched in to help. Eve had already begun sousing the muddy garments in the water.

"That," Joel explained, "was Colonel Lemuel Hampton. He says he was the first claimant of this lot, and he is going to have the law on me. He was the stagecoach agent here before the run."

With bitter endurance, Joel drove the shelter tent's stake deep in fresh grass-matted sod while Britt heaved around on the tautening rope.

"The fact is," Joel lowered his voice, "he's not only a Sooner. He's a greedy Sooner. He says he has influence. I expect he does. He's been here for months. The day before the run he staked this lot, the adjoining lot there on the corner, and the corner lot across the street."

Eve straightened up, and stood thoughtfully alongside the wash bucket.

"A soldier standing sentry duty over there in front of the land office saw him," Joel said. "Now Hampton is claiming one lot in his name, one in Lang's name, and the other—what's his lawyer's name?"

"Nash," Eve recalled.

Joel nodded. "Three of the best lots in town. The corner lot here and the one across the street are still empty. Nothing on them but the name stakes Hampton drove last Sunday."

Eve was calling, "Hey! You! Buddy." She was walking toward a nondescript boomer who stood with snuff-pouched jaw, engaged in talk with a group of idling men. "What'll you take to scoot across there to the land office and tell Colonel Lemuel Hampton that all three of his claims just got jumped?"

She swung, informing Britt, "I'll take the one yonder across the street. You take the corner lot here next to Joel's," Eve ordered Britt. She glanced at the laundry bucket, "I'll get that finished afterwhile," and returned impatient attention to the lanky snuff-chewer, "Well, buddy?"

His grimace exposed yellowed teeth. "Hell, I like runnin' errands for purty ladies." He started across the street, hesitating to call back to his companions, "Boys, this likely might stir some excitement."

Eve urged, "Don't wait," and headed with long strides for the far lot.

Britt looked thoughtfully at Joel.

"If you can't reach the apples," Joel shrugged, "shake the tree!"

Feeling like a watch officer who had just sighted the masts of a privateer hull down over the horizon, Britt walked onto the adjoining lot.

Hampton, Nash, and Lang came out of the land office with the snuff-chewer alongside. Squinting into the sun, the boomer pointed out Britt, then Eve.

Across the intersection Eve leaned, working the claim stake back and forth in the sod earth. It came free and she staggered backward, regaining balance and raising the stake to shield her eyes against the bright nooning sun as she stared at the land office.

Bits of sod dropped off the claim stake. Eve, certain that Hampton, Nash, and Lang saw her, heaved the stake with a contemptuous two-handed throw into the street. She dusted clinging bits of sod from her palms.

Britt held the stake he pulled from the sod long enough to read its declaration. It declared that the legal claimant to the lot on which he stood was Matthew Lang, aged thirty-six, a citizen of the United States. Judging accurately, Britt tossed the stake out to land in the street alongside Eve's.

The colonel and his hired men still stood three abreast, in front of the land office. The crowd gathering left a wide, funneling lane open for Hampton, Lang, and Nash to use in crossing the street.

Britt decided that while Colonel Hampton's broadcloth suit

was expensive, the man should be classified as a rube. Hampton held his narrow-brimmed felt hat in hand, his pale, rice-straw hair blown and disarranged by the wind. His face was one that would be forever sun-burned and peeling, with rough shaggy splotches of shedding skin.

Hampton's powerful, thick body was solid, not flaccid or corpulent. He was not town soft. His thickness was the ungainly, tough, powerful shape earned on a farm, working behind a binder, pitching bundles from first light to dark. An awkward shape which no suit, ready-made from store rack, or hand-cut and tailored, could ever trim and improve.

From Hampton's ungainly, round-shouldered shape Britt turned his attention to Matt Lang. Lang's chest, framed by the wide suspenders which exaggerated its outthrust, was as formidable as his tireless-looking boss.

Britt looked at youthful, slight Joel Decatur, and said, "How are you at marlinspike seamanship?"

Joel replied, "What?"

"Never mind." Britt concentrated his attention on the three men at the narrow end of the funnel.

The three entered the funnel, spreading apart as they came. The lawyer, hanging a little behind the other two, walked with a spraddled gait as though his pants were too tight in the crotch. Britt figured him for a bully covering deep fears, entering this encounter only because it was three to two.

Hampton took off his coat. Britt shed his uniform jacket. Britt's years as a midshipman and junior officer had made him hard-muscled. His heart was pumping now with excitement. Scrambling over high-masted rigging, the monkey-life of a mid-shipman on a square-rigger, had been good training. Even now, as a junior officer at sea, he ran the ratlines. Seaworthiness is a first lieutenant's responsibility, and Britt aimed that no grudge-holding sailor filled with Dutch courage on shore liberty should ever figure him as an easy mark. It was not unusual for a soft officer to be scuttled in some alley. Britt was determined that every man he commanded should be certain that he gave no order he could not carry out himself.

Hampton, Lang, and Nash strode on Joel's lot and split apart. Hampton and Nash hung their coats on the forward pole of Joel's shelter tent. Lang unslung his gunbelt and hung it there. Hampton headed for Joel. Lang and Nash, ten yards apart, came at Britt.

Leaning sharply to duck Lang's first roundhouse swing, Britt put a shoulder in Lang's belly, and hoisted. Bucking, Lang went up, then down, to land with a grunt on the flat of his back. Nash threw a handful of dirt that stung Britt's eyelids. Eyes shut, Britt swung a kick aimed to land where he hoped Nash's softest guts were.

Then he opened his eyes to see how Joel was making out. Decatur was agile, Hampton hard after him. The colonel howled for Joel to stand and fight. The consequences, if Hampton got his hands on Joel, made Britt hurry. Lang was picking himself up. Britt ran past him. Quentin Nash was leaning over his kicked belly, his face blood red and pain tortured, but he managed to stick out one fat leg in an attempt to trip Britt.

In fights on foreign wharves, leverages and chopping blows were ancient skills—unfamiliar to this land-locked prairie. Britt cut at the lawyer's fat leg and delivered a sidelong kick intended to benumb Nash. The lawyer spraddled, falling awkwardly and staying where he fell, bent in an unfamiliar attitude.

Matt Lang came at Britt from behind, grabbing him and swinging him clear of the ground. Britt went completely limp, then exploded in a thrash that broke the gunman's grip. Free, Britt launched a heel in a mule-like backward kick.

The solid landing of the kick was followed by the thud of Lang's head hitting the sod, audible even over the shouts of the rooting crowd. Lang had had enough of that. He rolled on his side to rest as Hampton captured Joel.

Colonel Lemuel Hampton gripped Decatur's shoulders and stood spread-legged, shaking the lighter Joel viciously. Joel's head was snapping back and forth with each shake. Wondering what kept Joel's neck from breaking, Britt ran on across the lot toward the struggling pair.

Quentin Nash now crawled up, half standing, and went reeling toward Lang's holstered revolver on the shelter tent stake. Britt went on toward Hampton and Decatur. Matt Lang got up, belligerently shaking off his dizziness. He came across the lot to fling Nash aside and jerk his revolver out of the holster. Britt had doubted that the lawyer, however hurt, had sufficiently lost his sense to gun down unarmed men, but he suspected that Lang, even though it meant the hang rope, was furious enough to shoot an unarmed man as if he were a dog in the street.

Joel Decatur would have to take care of himself as best he could. Britt altered his course to encounter Lang, but it was too late. The gunman had his weapon. Then Eve appeared before Lang like the threatening angel of death. She was pointing the shotgun Britt had seen on the shelf beneath Roody's bank counter.

She did not speak, but Matt Lang interrupted his charge to glare rather stupidly into the double-barrels of the shotgun. Confronted by Eve's weapon of bloody slaughter, he dropped the revolver.

The lawyer sat in torpor on the ground where Lang had shoved him. Nash groaned, kneading his fat belly. Seeing the revolver fall from Lang's hand, Eve said quietly, "That is a good boy. Back off now and leave it." When Lang hesitated, she added grimly, "I'll blow your head off!"

Britt moved on in behind Hampton. He wrapped an arm and elbow around Hampton's neck and levered up the burly colonel's chin. Lifting a knee into Hampton's back, Britt heaved, then wondered what kept Hampton's neck from breaking. The man was as strong as an ox.

Britt shifted his hip under the small of Hampton's back. Pivoting then, Britt used his elbow as a sledge, driving Hampton's face mercilessly earthward. Hampton's meaty hands came loose from Joel's shoulders. Decatur reeled backward to stand giddy and wobbling.

Hampton, bent back over Britt's hip, was trying to raise his arms to protect his face from the battering elbow. He seemed harmless. Britt let him go.

It was a mistake. The colonel was a bulldog. He recovered his balance and was coming on to attack when the shotgun's double barrels greeted him. Hampton retreated back, crouched like a threatening bear hardly hindered by his predicament.

Eve ordered briskly, "Joel, take the bullets out of that pistol."

Joel, his eyes wobbling, sought to fix his gaze on the ground and the pistol. Britt picked up Lang's heavy .45. He snapped open the cylinder, punched the cartridges out, and tossed the weapon to Lang.

Hampton, taking out his handkerchief, stobbed at his nose to staunch the flow of blood from his nostrils. "I warn you, sir," he told Britt in handkerchief-muffled passion, "I am going to arm myself. I warn you. Do the same. I'll kill you on sight."

Lang stepped toward the tent pole-hung gunbelt. Eve hypnotized him with a threatening gesture of her shotgun. She said, "Joel!"

Decatur, his eyes still wobbling like loosened oarlocks, was leaning on the tent pole. He took down the gunbelt. Carefully removing each cartridge, dropping them in the dust, Joel tossed the belt to Lang.

Quentin Nash, painfully rubbing and nursing the hurts on his fat body, fell in behind Colonel Lemuel Hampton now as Hampton stormed off the lot, wadding his bloody handkerchief and swabbing at his bloody face.

Matt Lang stood cynically alone. Wearing an expression of ironic bravado he strapped on the empty-looped belt. Holstering his gun, as if he did this of his own choice, and in his own good time, he followed Hampton and Nash.

Roody came running through the gap left by the trio's departure. He looked around, saw Eve, and yelled wildly, "Idiot!"

He ran to her and pulled the shotgun out of her hands. His wiggy hair quivering, as if each hair had an independent will, Roody turned, hands trembling, to Britt: "She ran in and grabbed it before I could stop her."

Roody broke open the shotgun's breech. Both barrels were empty. The shotgun had not been loaded.

"I had to lock the safe and lock the outside door before I could come," Roody jibbered in frenzied apology. "I couldn't leave people's money just standing there, wide open, to be stolen."

Britt looking thoughtfully at the unloaded shotgun, turned his attention to Eve. She seemed undisturbed. She smiled artlessly and lifted her fingers in a shrugging, baffled gesture.

She likes to bluff, Britt thought; her profanity, the invitation into her Pullman berth, somehow the empty shotgun seemed related to both. Her immodesty as she humiliated the Arkansas City store clerk, her baiting of Roody, Britt wondered if she was all bluff, if her shotgun was ever loaded?

Roody was staring at him, as if expecting some comment on Eve's behavior. The more Britt thought about the empty shotgun and the comparison that had at first seemed so brilliant, the less sensible it seemed.

She was no kitten masquerading in a wildcat's skin. If Lang had succeeded in getting his hands on his revolver, Eve Andrews would have pulled the trigger on that shotgun. Of this Britt felt very sure, and if it had been loaded there would have been a headless gunman in Logan Station.

Roody teetered impatiently, glaring at Britt. Then, muttering, red-faced and frustrated, Roody gave up and left. Carrying his shotgun, he disappeared in the milling crowd heading back toward his bank.

"We should have kept that shotgun," Eve said.

Joel grinned. "You can't beat an unloaded shotgun for dispelling a crisis."

"For postponing a crisis," Britt said.

Eve said thoughtfully, "You've got that gun of Dink Casey's in your war bag."

"In my seabag," he corrected her.

"Where can you get a gun?" she asked Joel.

"I don't want a gun," Joel demurred. "This contest will have to be settled in court. When I go to court I'd rather be a claimant, not on trial for a killing."

"You can't go to court if you're dead," Eve declared.

"If I'm dead, I won't be worried about a thing," Joel said smiling. "I'll just stand on my rights, and see what happens."

"Unarmed?" Eve was incredulous.

"Unarmed," Joel nodded.

Eve made a disappointed mouth. She lifted the sagging entrance flap of Joel's shelter tent, pulled a quilt out of the heap of rumpled bedding inside, and walked back across the street to the corner lot, lugging the quilt in her arms. Reaching the lot, she folded the quilt, placed it on the ground and sat on it.

Imperturbably, Joel reset the uprooted tent stake, patiently tightened the rope, then turned to Britt to ask: "Do you think she's right?"

"About what?"

"That they'll be back."

"Hampton sure sounded determined," Britt speculated.

"The lots are valuable, all right," Joel mused. "But to be willing to kill for them—"

"Seems unlikely," Britt agreed. "There are too many witnesses hereabouts."

Joel nodded. "If we arm ourselves, and permit them to goad us into action that would let them claim self-defense—"

"It could get a little bloody," Britt said.

Joel shook his head. "I can't take that route. I'd rather lose the lot."

"Seems like a poor way to start a town."

"How do you mean?" Joel asked.

"To turn it over to the bully boys right away," Britt said firmly.

"You're a fighting man," Joel's face was grave, "but for our country. Not for me."

"What's the difference?" Britt persisted.

"This is a private quarrel."

"Right's right. Private quarrel or otherwise."

Joel stood silent, and uncertain.

"What say I go sit down on that other lot for a while?" Britt suggested. "Let's see what happens."

Joel looked across at the waiting and expectant Eve. "Providing—if they come, you'll let me make the decision whether to stick or quit."

"Fine," Britt said. "But she won't quit." He nodded toward Eve.

Joel stood without reply. Britt waited a moment, then walked onto the adjoining lot.

Minutes passed. Britt stood awhile, and then sat down.

A quarter hour became a half hour, and turned to boredom. The afternoon sun was hot.

Eve called out, "I'm thirsty."

Joel, carrying water bucket and dipper, left his lot to cross the street.

Britt saw Eve peer down into the bucket.

"Not your laundry water," she protested.

"It's not," Britt heard Joel reply.

"The color this stuff is," she insisted, "there could be anything down there. I can't see the bottom of the bucket."

"It's river water," Joel laughed. "A little riley, but clean."

"It wasn't this muddy yesterday."

"I think it must have rained somewhere upstream last night," Joel explained. "Go on, drink it," he urged. "This water has character. It will stick to your ribs."

She drank it. "Tastes all right." She handed the dipper to Joel. "I'm hungry. Let's go get something to eat. No one's coming."

Britt could see the look of clear relief on Joel's face as Eve stood up and glanced downhill, then she said, "Oh, oh!"

Hampton, Nash, and Lang were half a block down the street. As they came determinedly up the hill Joel dropped the dipper back into the water bucket and returned grim-lipped to his lot.

Britt could see the glint of a metal badge pinned on Lang's left suspender long before they reached the lot. It had not been there when he had last seen the gunman. The three men passed Eve as if she did not exist. They came to the edge of Joel's lot, and stopped there.

Nash stood pompously. Lang's arms hung slack at his sides, his face dull. The metal badge pinned on his suspender was a silver star. The loops of the gunman's leather belt had been filled. It sagged heavily with leather cartridges.

Colonel Hampton had washed his face. It was no longer bloody. In spite of a swollen nose the arrogance of his bearing was apparent.

Britt watched quietly, seeing no evidence that Hampton was armed in spite of his threat. Nash's rumpled white sack suit could have concealed an arsenal. Lang stood as expressionless as a cold side of meat hung in a butcher shop. He made no move toward his gun. Quentin Nash looked at Hampton.

Hampton nodded.

Nash, horsey and pompous, said, "I have the duty to inform you that the people of Logan Station have just held a town meeting at the railroad depot and Mr. Lang has been elected marshal. You, all three of you"—he looked carefully at Britt, Joel, and Eve—"are under arrest for seizing lots which are the legal property of Colonel Hampton, Marshal Lang, and myself."

Joel looked across the distance separating the lots at Britt. With a beckoning gesture of his head Britt started across the lot toward Nash.

The lawyer stood his ground to demand, "Will you submit peaceably to arrest?"

Eve, coming across the street, asked loudly, "How could any-body elect a stupid thug like that to be marshal?"

The silver star hanging on Lang's suspender was engraved *CITY MARSHAL*. Britt could read the words as he approached.

Joel, ignoring Hampton, Nash, and Lang, said to Britt, "There must be ten thousand people on this townsite. We didn't know what was happening at the depot."

Britt and Eve exchanged glances, and Eve admitted, "We knew about the meeting. Nate Richter told Britt and me this morning."

"Well," Joel said thoughtfully, "we're at a disadvantage be-fore the law." After a moment's concentration he told Nash, "We'll submit to arrest, but not to confinement. Will you take us before the magistrate?"

As they followed Hampton across the street toward the land office, Eve declared, "It was stupid to forget that meeting. If we'd been at the depot—"

"Hampton would have taken possession of my lot," said Joel.

"It's heads they win, tails we lose," Eve decided.

Nash and Hampton, busy with talk, were lagging behind, leading the prisoners to the dull-faced Lang. As they entered the land office Joel nodded a greeting to the sentry on the door. They filed on through the land office to a room at the rear. It was rigged as a courtroom.

Nash and Hampton faded back into a corner. The United States flag stood beside the low rostrum from which the judge presided and Britt experienced a mild surprise.

The presiding magistrate was the same pendulous-jowled Judge Roland Trumbull who had burst in portly hurry from the washroom on the train from St. Louis, to collide with Britt.

The judge interrupted a conference with his bailiff to stare at Britt.

"Lieutenant," Judge Trumbull's bullfrog voice graveled. "Am I to take it that you are under arrest?"

"It appears that I am," Britt admitted.

In the far corner of the courtroom Nash and Hampton still huddled, their backs prominent as they bent their heads together in conspiratorial whispering. Britt saw Colonel Hampton glance toward Eve and he saw Nash's covert thumb gesture toward her. Whatever they were up to, it would somehow focus on Eve.

Trumbull scrutinized the star pinned on Matt Lang's suspender. "What is your status, sir?" he asked curiously.

Quentin Nash now hurried up from the rear of the courtroom to reply, "Your honor, Mr. Lang is the newly elected Marshal of Logan Station."

"And yours?" The judge transferred his attention to Nash.

"I am attorney of record representing Colonel Lemuel Hampton, Mr. Lang in his capacity as a private citizen, and myself."

"What is the charge?"

"These three have unlawfully pre-empted the claims of Colonel Hampton, Mr. Lang, and myself."

Colonel Hampton stood stiffly behind Nash's left shoulder, grimly eying Eve. Judge Trumbull thoughtfully surveyed the entire assemblage, and turned his attention to Britt.

"Lieutenant, what do you have to say about all this?"

Britt raised his shoulders. "The claims were deserted, your honor. We just moved onto them."

Joel added, "We'll certainly plead not guilty to any charge of claim jumping."

"Hmmmm," the judge mused. "Well, let's get on with it."

"Your honor," Nash volunteered, "these cases are identical. May I propose that we choose one from the three and let the decision in it stand sufficient for all?"

Judge Trumbull mulled this. "Yes, well." He looked uncertainly at Britt, Eve and Joel. "What would be your reaction to that?"

Britt decided it was time for them to confer. He said to Judge Trumbull, "Sir, could we talk this over?"

The judge nodded and Britt led Eve and Joel to the same corner where Hampton and Nash had huddled.

"What are they up to?" Eve hissed.

Decatur shrugged. "I have no idea."

"Whatever it is," Britt assured her, "you're going to be right in the middle of it."

"Let me just tell them to go to—" Her voice was rising to the point of clear audibility in the small courtroom and Joel gestured vaguely for caution.

"They're taking a gamble," Joel reasoned. "They think they've got something that makes their case a cinch." He paused. "Of course it may be a cinch that if we can't win one of these cases we're unlikely to win any of them. I'm inclined to go along. Maybe we can catch onto their game, whatever it is, before they get the case nailed down too tight." He turned to lead the way back up to the judge's bench.

"We will agree," Joel said, "to trying one case and let it stand for all three."

Judge Trumbull cleared his throat. "Do you wish an attorney to plead for you?" he asked.

"I am an attorney, your honor," said Joel.

"Do you wish a postponement—"

"Your honor," Nash said hastily, "we move that the case be heard and settled immediately."

Judge Hampton looked at Joel.

Joel nodded. "Agreed."

"In that case," said Trumbull, "we'll proceed. Which case shall we try?"

"I move, your honor," said Nash, "that we adhere to the age-old adage 'ladies first.'" Quentin Nash bowed formally toward Eve.

"Who is the disputing claimant in the young lady's case?" Judge Trumbull asked.

"I, your honor." Nash bowed to the judge.

Then Joel took the initiative. "We are agreeable, your honor. We do, however, request trial by jury."

Colonel Lemuel Hampton, who had seated himself comfortably in a chair at the long table fronting the bench, leaped up.

"Your honor." Hampton's stubborn voice spoke the title grudgingly. The stolid belligerence of the man was strongly evident. "I want to say that justice has to move fast on a frontier like this. We've got no time for such foolishness as juries. If you don't take care you'll have your docket dragging so far behind—"

Judge Trumbull's gavel rapped once, sharply. "Order, here. I'm competent to run my court, sir. You sit down and speak through your counsel, or remain silent." He turned to Joel. "There has not yet been a trial by jury in this Territory. We have no provisions for empaneling a jury."

Decatur's face was set determinedly. "Your honor, we have no right to deny Miss Andrews a trial by jury."

Hampton was on his feet again, this time with a hoarse but unintelligible shout.

The judge's pounding gavel expressed the anger which was taking hold of his features. He pointed the heavy end of the gavel directly at Hampton. "Sir, any more from you and you will be cited for contempt. I'll determine how much haste will be allowed in these proceedings."

Judge Trumbull lowered his angry voice to address Joel Decatur. "We have no arrangement to pay jury fees. I can't empanel a jury and compel it to act without compensation."

Through the windows at the sides of the courtroom Britt could see the crowd gathering to listen. Faces in it were beginning to seem familiar. It appeared to be about the same group of onlookers who had observed the struggle seesaw back and forth since Nash and Lang's first attack on Joel yesterday.

They had watched Hampton throw Joel's laundry in the street. They had watched the attack that Eve had finally settled with the unloaded shotgun. This same crowd had heard the three claim jumpers' continued threats of violence. Britt suddenly understood Joel's insistence on a jury trial.

Removing six silver dollars from his pocket, Britt stepped forward and stacked them on Judge Trumbull's desk. "There's the jury fees, your honor."

Colonel Hampton was half out of his chair but Nash managed to seize his shoulder. "Your honor." Nash worked at forcing the colonel back into his chair.

"Yes, counseler?" the judge queried.

"I must object," Nash protested, "most strenuously. This is the first time in all my knowledge of criminal jurisprudence that I have seen a defendant openly undertake to buy a jury even before it is empaneled."

"Be seated, sir," Trumbull ordered gruffly. "I've rendered no opinion here. Please give the names of the disputants and the claim location to the bailiff."

A framed copy of the United States Constitution hung on a wall peg behind Judge Trumbull's swivel chair. While the bailiff took down names the judge swiveled his chair around to carefully study the framed document.

His chair squeaked gratingly as he swung around to announce his decision. "The young gentleman is correct. We have no right, under the Constitution of the United States, to deny trial by jury to any citizen."

Judge Trumbull received the bailiff's document. "We'll empanel a jury. You"—he consulted the bailiff's document and grumbled—"Mr. Nash—will have the privilege of striking three jurors, and you"—he glanced again at the list—"Mr. Decatur—may strike three."

Judge Roland Trumbull scribbled, then handed the document to his bailiff, "Here is the venire. Get that soldier at the guard post. Pick twelve men at random from the crowd outside."

As the jurors so hastily empaneled wandered in Judge Roland Trumbull seated them, inquiring their occupations. Three were gamblers, one was a hardware drummer. Seven were emigrant settlers, and one unshaven, toothless old man stated that he had no occupation.

"We're selecting a Common Pleas jury of six, gentlemen,"

Judge Trumbull told the group. "The attorneys may proceed."

Quentin Nash moved to exclude three of the emigrant settlers. Joel struck off the three gamblers, leaving four settlers, the hardware salesman, and the rheumy-eyed old man who sat listening eagerly, his hand cupped to his ear.

Nash arose to state his case.

His voice rose with oratorical fervor and sweeping gestures. "This girl's case will be based on her supposition that I am a 'Sooner.' Whereas I can prove beyond the shadow of any doubt that I arrived here only yesterday, on the fourth train from Arkansas City, on the afternoon of that historic day—Monday, April 22, 1889."

Nash sat down, his strategy now plain to Britt. It would be easy enough for Nash to prove when he arrived. It would then be equally easy, Britt knew, for Nash to call witnesses whose testimony would prove that Eve had "jumped his claim." Many in the crowd around the courtroom had seen her pull up Nash's stake and take possession of his claim only a few hours ago. Probably someone sitting on the jury had seen her. Not only had she jumped Nash's claim, but she had done it with flamboyance, evidently to provoke trouble.

Joel, approaching the bench to open his case, addressed the judge: "Your honor, the point in contention here is not when the litigants arrived. It is when the lot was staked. The stake was driven before any train arrived. And not even by Nash. The lot was staked several days before the run, by Colonel Hampton, who was already here as an agent of the L.S. & W. Stagecoach Line."

Hampton and Nash exchanged a covert glance. Hampton was clearly still seething with anger from the judge's earlier censure as Nash hastily arose to say, "Your honor, I would like to call as my first witness Mr. Matt Lang, who as the elected marshal of this city is an officer of this court."

Matt Lang took the stand and was sworn by the bailiff.

"Now, Mr. Lang," Nash began. "Can you testify as to the time of my arrival here in Logan Station?"

"Yes, sir," Lang replied. "It was getting on toward two o'clock, yesterday afternoon."

"And how can you be sure of this?" Nash asked.

"Why, I was riding on the train with you," Lang declared.

Nash smirked visibly. "And that would have been on the twenty-second day of this month, April 1889."

"It sure would."

"Thank you, Marshal Lang," Nash concluded. "Unless the defense counsel has some question, you may step down."

Joel shook his head, and Matt Lang swaggered back to his seat at Hampton's table.

"I would now like to call Colonel Lemuel Hampton," said Nash.

When the belligerently stubborn Hampton was seated beside the judge and sworn, Nash deliberately phrased his first question.

"Colonel, would you tell the court when you first learned that this defendant, I believe her name is Eve Andrews, when you first learned that Miss Andrews had illegally taken possession of your claim—in the vernacular, 'jumped your claim'?"

Joel Decatur was on his feet now. "Your honor, I object to this line of questioning," he protested. "First things first. The first thing that must be established here is when the stake claiming that lot was driven into the ground, and who drove it!"

"Your honor," Nash began intoning . . .

Judge Trumbull's gavel whacked once. "Counsel for the defense is correct. Objection sustained."

The judge leaned forward, his fingers rotating the gavel. "Colonel"—his eyes traveled down the paper on his desk— "Hampton. Do you wish to testify as to when you staked the lot?"

With a throat sound inchoate as an angered bear Hampton

lurched up out of the witness chair, "In this kangaroo court? I'll—"

Trumbull's gavel cracked like a pistol shot. "I find you in contempt!" the judge declared. "You will pay the bailiff a fine of ten dollars before leaving this courtroom." He turned to address the jury: "Gentlemen, since it seems that the plaintiff in this case is unable, or unwilling, to attempt to prove when the lot was staked, this case seems ready to go to the jury. If in your opinion the plaintiff here did not have legal possession of that lot, you cannot find this defendant, Eve Andrews, guilty of claim jumping. Is the defendant guilty or not guilty?"

A lean immigrant settler looked down the line at his fellow jurors. "Boys, what do you say?"

The jurors conferred in brief whispers, and the settler who had chosen himself jury foreman arose.

"She ain't guilty," he told Judge Trumbull.

As Joel, Eve, and Britt filed out of the courtroom, Britt heard Judge Trumbull say to Colonel Hampton, "I believe you stated, sir, that justice has to move fast on a frontier like this. Was that fast enough for you?"

The sun cast a long shadow across the lot from Joel's shelter tent. In the shade of it sat Eve, Britt, Joel, the Reverend Obadiah Quigley, and the preacher's newly arrived young wife.

Cherry McDowell Quigley had arrived on the train from Nacogdotches, a winsome, soft-voiced creature far from Britt's idea of a preacher's wife. Her presence seemed even to temper Eve's rash manners.

The low sun, near setting, and after-supper lassitude kept conversation slow.

Music from the Stutz and Basil brass band carried up the hill. The pans and tin cups on the grass around them were empty.

"A clear day tomorrow," Eve commented.

"Empty dishes are fine for proverbs," Joel said, "but they have to be washed."

"We won't worry about that for the moment," the Reverend Quigley smiled.

Cherry Quigley's style was gentle, and what she said came out, "Youah not worrin' 'bout it at all. Eve and I'll have to wash them."

Eve said shortly, "I hate washing dishes."

The preacher told Eve: "Your willfulness is noteworthy. I've been afraid you might force me to wash them."

"So that's why you've been looking so apprehensive," thrust Eve.

The preacher, eying the activity in the Stutz and Basil tent down the hill, said, "Well, not really. About a block from here are thirty ladies of the W.C.T.U., as primed and eager as an Irish marching club. Somehow I've got to persuade them not to march."

Eve, reluctantly, began gathering pans.

Cherry Quigley joined her, lifting a half-filled bucket of water from the embers of the campfire. She set it on a camp stool and tested the temperature of the water gingerly.

Joel suggested, "I thought you'd be encouraging the ladies to march, and joining them in their crusade, Reverend."

"Cherry and I attended a protracted meeting down south a few weeks ago," Quigley said. "The evangelist kept preaching, 'Get your life in tune with God!' What he should have been preaching was 'Attune your life to creative power.' If you are to accomplish, you must be tuned to create, not to destroy. Those W.C.T.U. ladies need to occupy themselves with some creative project and stop trying to destroy evil."

Cherry Quigley came to touch her husband's shoulder. "Obadiah, don't you think you should save your preachments for Sunday?"

The young preacher had to conclude his thought. "Evil tends to destroy itself," he declared. "The only effective way to defeat evil is to be creative.

"Healthy grass will crowd out weeds. A busy, useful life will crowd out evil. It does not require purging so much as scrutiny through meditation and setting in order through prayer."

He looked around then, at his wife, and blushed. "I'm sorry. I shouldn't be sermonizing here."

"Don't apologize," Britt said. "I'll be gone before Sunday. I should have the opportunity to hear at least one of your sermons."

Quigley's blush was cherubic. "At least it was short. Perhaps I can use it to persuade the ladies to abandon their onslaught on the Stutz and Basil tent."

Cherry Quigley suggested: "Perhaps you can persuade them to use their energy in making a church canvass of Logan Station. That would aid in getting the church established here, and they'll feel they've accomplished something before returning to their homes."

Impatiently, Eve asked, "Where do you want these pans, Joel?"

"Just stack them inside the corner of the tent, please," he said.

Eve's tartness impelled Britt to direct a covert glance at her. Quigley queried Britt, "When are you leaving?"

"Tomorrow," Britt said. "Northbound aboard the same train your wife arrived on today. I'll reach the West Coast on Sunday."

From the tent flap Eve asked, "What are you doing tonight?"

"Turning in early," Britt said. "We've been getting barely enough sleep for survival."

His reply was an angry clatter of pans inside Joel's tent.

With the polite wishes for a restful night the group broke up. Britt arose to escort Eve downhill to the Evans tents.

Cherry Quigley said, "Oh, Eve, I finished reading this on the train. Perhaps you'd enjoy looking at it before you go to sleep." She handed Eve an issue of *Godey's Ladies Book*.

Eve said, "Thank you." Her smile was not enthusiastic.

When Britt had left her, Eve sat on the edge of the cot in her tent room, desultorily flipping through the pages of the magazine.

She tossed the *Ladies Book* aside and sat fidgeting, listening to the sounds of activity outside the Evans tents. Harness jingled on passing teams. Boot heels tramped by on earth made hard by an unending human procession along the narrow, street side path. Building activity provided an unremitting restless backdrop of cacophonic noise.

The galloping hoofs of horses approached, and passed the tent. With impatience, Eve dragged the single wooden chair in the tent room over to the canvas sidewall.

She climbed on the chair to peer out through the narrow gap between the sidewall and top of the tent. She gripped the sidewall then, pulling it down to enlarge her view. Like a prisoner staring out through cell bars, she watched the activity down the block toward the Stutz and Basil tent.

In the evening dusk the hanging lamps of the gambling tent glowed pale and opalescent, spilling their cones of light over the gaming tables and the men playing at them.

The tune of the band's quickstep livened the air. From the Evans tent room, the Floradora girls dancing yonder on the stage seemed like small flesh-tinted puppets. Atop the piano in front of the stage, Eve could see the diminutive figure of Peardeedo. She could make out the shape of his guitar, clasped beneath his arm.

With brisk decision then, Eve jumped down off the chair and left the tent.

13

Effusively, courteously, Roody saw the last bank customer out. He closed the door, locked it, and abandoned his dignity as a banker. Roody leaned against the door muttering, and wearily shut his eyes.

He dropped the door key in one vest pocket and pulled his watch from the other.

"Six o'clock." He snorted derisively, "Banker's hours!"

The bank had been as busy as the land office, but Roody's elation was dulled by aching legs.

He calculated thoughtfully, and told himself aloud, "I've been on my feet for more than twelve hours."

Droopy with fatigue he sagged across to the deposit counter, threw a leg up and climbed to sit on it. He pulled off his shoes. They dropped in noisy succession and Roody lay down lengthwise on the counter, staring at the ceiling. He closed his eyes, but they crept open. He wiggled his toes.

I'm strung up as nervous as a cat in the dog pound, he thought.

Swinging down off the counter he went to the safe. For a moment he surveyed the neatly stacked currency, heaped sacks of miscellaneous silver, wrapped rolls of gold coins, packets of drafts, documents bundled with twine, the folded money belt, the metallic gray locked jewelry box.

Roody reached behind the jewelry box and lifted out a pint bottle of whiskey. It was nearly full. He took a long pull, wiped his mouth, and muttered aloud, "For medicinal purposes."

He sat down on the floor, cross-legged in front of the safe, considering its contents with fixed eyes. "I'm going to have to make a money shipment to Kansas City," he informed himself, and took another pull on the bottle.

The whiskey primed his digestive juices and warmed his empty belly.

"Whew," he muttered as the whiskey hit suddenly and his head began to swim.

Roody climbed back up on the counter, lay on his back and dozed for three quarters of an hour. When he opened his eyes, he murmured, "That's better," but now his back muscles were stiff from the hardness of the countertop.

He sat up to knead the muscles and ask himself, "Why didn't I go back in the back room and lay on the cot?"

Then he remembered. The money shipment. If he had gone to sleep on the cot he probably would have slept all night. He got down to resume his cross-legged seat before the safe and once more primed his pipes from the whiskey bottle.

"Irish whiskey," Roody said admiringly, "the best medicine."

He had another drink, stood up, his head promptly reeled, and he leaned against the counter.

"Whew! Maybe I'd better go get something to eat."

He placed his ledgers in the safe, closed and locked it, and fumbled for the door key in his vest pocket.

Outside, he counted his pocket change in the dusky light. Two dollars and eighty-three cents. *Damn. Well, in such a state of affairs,* he thought, *the Stutz and Basil free-lunch counter seems to be the best bet.* Roody struck out across the crest of the hill, cutting through the block of camp sites to arrive at the gambling tent.

A double shot of bourbon to further prime the digestive processes. Then with shot glass in hand he made his way to the free lunch at the end of the bar to nibble a boiled egg while he watched the early evening show on stage.

Seeing it all through the pleasant hue of bourbon, the Floradora girls aroused his male instincts. The sentimental songs of Inez Basil were especially moving.

In warm emotional turmoil, Roody left his empty glass on the bar and made his way through the crowd as soon as the performance ended. He greeted Inez Basil as she emerged from the dressing cubicle.

"Beautiful, dear lady," he declared, looking earnestly up at her. "Your voice is a delight."

She smiled down at him, "Why, thank you, Mr. Andrews."

"Might I have the privilege of buying you a drink?"

Inez glanced at her husband, busy at the wheel. "I think so," she said. "Why not?"

Roody sensed the attention of envious eyes as he escorted this attractive woman to the bar. Her acceptance of his first invitation prompted a second. His pocket-fumbling to pay for the second caused a rise of chagrin.

Requesting credit sharpened Roody's embarrassment. Inez was forced to explain, in equally great embarrassment, that her husband was adamantly insistent that no one, however responsible, be permitted to establish a bar bill in the saloon.

Roody could not allow himself even the satisfaction of a sharp rejoinder. It was senseless to blame a lovely woman for the penuriousness of a dull husband.

Hurriedly, Roody returned to the bank. He spent a brief time in front of the safe, for he knew that the contents of the money belt were exactly recorded in the ledger. He would need to make only a simple mathematical calculation to replace any small amount he might use from the money belt.

So Roody, his staggering hardly noticeable, pulled out his shirt tail, strapped the boomer's money belt next to his drawers, swung shut the safe door and hurried out.

The hard swung safe door created a pneumatic effect inside the safe. The heavy steel door rebounded only slightly from the air cushion it formed, the air escaping soundlessly from the thin gap, but there was no locking click.

Roody locked the front door carefully, vest-pocketed the door key, and hurried back to the Stutz and Basil tent. His apology to Inez was effusive and sincere. Though somewhat fuzzy, Roody felt a yearning need to offer her a bit more entertainment to make up for the embarrassment he had caused by leaving her at the bar. She considered his request with sweet feminine courtesy, and suggested that a game of chance might offer divertissement.

"Perhaps"—her smile was touched with sad irony—"I'll bring you luck."

As the liquor eased his weariness, the earth seemed softer. His thoughts floated entirely free and clear, and Roody knew his mind was sharply alert in the smoky, timeless haze that seemed to fill the gambling tent.

It was at times like these that he was at his best. The distinctly heard clicks of the chips—checks—as the monte dealer changed the bets on the dim lit green table reassured Roody that he was entirely sober.

He certainly felt no animosity toward her. Roody could not permit himself to shift the blame to Inez as he lost. She stood tirelessly beside his chair. Just damned bad luck that no one could have changed. Which was proved by the fact that his luck grew worse during the intervals when Inez left the table for her successive performances on stage during the evening.

Roody felt some emotional shock when she left the table for the night's last performance, for he realized how little money remained in the belt. He quit the game and ordered a double bourbon at the bar to bolster himself, to ease the shock, and felt that perhaps the last drink made him a little drunk.

Surely even the softness of the sawdust underfoot could hardly account for the lack of feeling in his extremities. He hardly seemed to be standing at all. The canvas roof of the tent seemed as billowy as if the wind had risen, but the roaring in his ears was not wind. And when Inez sang so sadly of the girl in the gilded cage Roody felt warm tears on his cheeks.

That cinched it. Roody knew he always became a bit over-emotional when drunk. At a time like this, Roody was not one to recoil from the truth, *by damn, I'm a little drunk,* he told himself, and as he stepped out across the tent toward the dressing cube—cubicle—his steps were long, long steps, and the floor of the tent receded with an unsteadying irregularity from his reaching feet. That, he took as humorous.

Laughingly, he explained his predicament to Inez, though the handicapping numbness of his lips provided something of a problem. Inez suggested that perhaps a drive in this rosy world, through the cool night air, might clear his head.

By damn, whoever—whenever—had Ro-o-dy Andrews been so fortunate? A lovely and congenial woman—why hell! He held her arm to escort her down the block. Roody fumbled through the money belt and paid for a rented rig with slippery money at the wagon yard. It was a good thing he helped her up into the buggy, Roody decided, or she might have fallen getting in. He did.

They rode out through shimmering campfires and the lantern lit streets of Logan Station into open country. It was a wonderful and unreal world. Roody was not sure where they were but the buggy seemed to float slowly through this beautiful night country. The air was chilly and refreshing on his hot face. He hoped in serene exaltation that he would be able to find this beautiful place again.

Inez moved against him. She was shivering, and her discomfort aroused his chivalric spirit.

"Lovely lady." His words echoed fulsomely, resonantly, in his own ears. Roody struggled to remove his coat which had somehow become stubborn and awkward to deal with.

He wrapped the reins loosely around his wrist and somehow the damned coat sleeve got off his arm and was sliding down the reins over the dashboard toward the team. In reaching after it the damned team must have made a lurch for he was leaning too far out over the dashboard and a horse tail switched his sweaty face.

Inez helped him. He felt her arms around his waist. She hauled him back into the buggy seat and Roody muttered his admiration for her alert help in what might have become a sadly dangerous situation. He placed the retrieved coat around her shoulders.

Being wet with sweat, the chill of the damp spring night made his teeth chatter violently. Graciously, Inez took the reins and let him lay his head in her lap as he explained his sympathy for her—being married to a penurious, granite-faced, unsympathetic husband as she was. Roody insisted that it was nothing at all when she welcomed his sympathy and his suggestion that he would be willing to offer her comfort whenever she felt the need of sympathy.

He must have dozed off while expressing this utter denunciation of George Basil, who was surely a problem for her. The motion of the buggy jarred him awake and Roody sympathized again, with eloquence. Her husband was a gambler, and Roody generously offered himself as a horrible example of the dangers of gambling. He became very sleepy while confessing with ashamed humility that he had lost some money tonight that really was not his own.

"Certainly I do not wish," Roody declared eloquently, "to burden a lady so gracious with the problems of my bad luck—"

When Inez offered to "take care of that for him" Roody did not want to become maudlin in his gratitude. He must have fallen soundly asleep, for it was extremely confusing to him when he woke up in silent dark in a motionless vehicle, which he presently determined was his own cot, in the back room of the clapboard Logan Station Commercial Bank.

Roody lay awake for a few moments. The cot was not utterly motionless for it seemed to rise and fall softly like a small boat rocking in a gentle sea. Roody once more marveled at how indebted he was to Inez for being so considerate. Feeling with his hands he determined that he was still fully dressed. Since that was so, he gave passing thought to getting up to check and balance his books and prepare the money shipment, but it was very dark and his head was still not as clear as he would like for it to be. Roody turned over and went back to sleep.

When he awakened the sunlight was hurting his eyes. A man, Dink Casey, was leaning over his cot. Dink Casey's revolver was drawn, and pointed straight at Roody's face.

14

Britt said doggedly: "Now let me understand this. Neither of you saw her leave."

"Why no." Mrs. Evans paused in stirring a pot of breakfast hominy grits. "She came in early last night, with you I think. If she left after that—"

Her husband, sliding plates along the plank table with his lone arm, suggested, "She may have gone out this morning before we got up."

"But you didn't hear her leave," Britt probed.

Mrs. Evans stirred briskly. "Her cot is still made up. Of course she could have done that this morning, before she left."

Four of the W.C.T.U. ladies came into the dining tent. One of them was Annette.

"I really don't think she slept here," Mrs. Evans explained. "I have a way of turning under the sheet corners . . . I just don't think Miss Andrews would be likely to do it exactly the same way."

Mrs. Chameau entered the dining tent.

Britt went over to the group. "Pardon me, ladies. Have any of you seen Miss Andrews since last night?"

"Miss Andrews?" Annette's mother seemed nonplused.

Annette reminded her. "Eve Andrews, Mother. The girl who was with Lieutenant Pierce—"

"Yes," Mrs. Chameau interrupted. "That bold girl who—oh, excuse me, I meant no reflection—no, we are planning to divide the entire town into districts this morning and canvass it to enumerate church memberships. Surely one of us will see her. Is there a message?"

"No. Thank you." Britt hurried back outside.

The seven o'clock sun was warming. Queerly, there seemed less activity in the street now than when he had first come down the hill from Joel's camp. The April morning mist rising from the river bottom hung in foggy whiteness in the hollows below the depot.

Britt walked a thoughtful half block to the corner. Ahead of him, centered in the next block, was the Stutz and Basil tent. It was shrouded in quiet, its sidewalls down.

Britt eyed the gambling tent, and thought of Peardeedo. Pensively, Britt started across the street. The odd quiet of the town, strongly evident now, was a silence more profound than any normal early morning ebb of activity. The febrile temper of it plucked at his attention. *She might have gone to see Peardeedo, last night,* he thought.

Surely not to see Joel. Certainly not Roody. If she had gone to Joel's camp, Britt puzzled, *even this morning, I would have encountered her somewhere on the way.* Britt looked up the hill. Then without completing his crossing, he stopped short.

The street toward the center of town was deserted. No wagon, no horse, no vehicle of any kind, moved in the empty street. The quiet was oppressive. No human, nothing alive moved. The lull up the hill was like a vacuum. Its absolute utter silence clamored in his ears as if it were a deafening sound.

It appeared to Britt like the eye of a hurricane at sea. He stared up the hill at the land office, in the center of the lull. Across the street from it stood the raw unpainted clapboard newness of Roody's bank.

The Logan Station Commercial Bank's canvas banner, broadly lettered, was billowing gently, like a slatting sail in the morning breeze. Its legend was visible only in successive parts, as the banner slatted, filling and emptying with the wind.

A man appeared, small at the far end of the block. He was

climbing out of the land office window. As he emerged he stood on the window sill, then hoisted himself up on the building's slanting roof. Another man appeared in the window, handing up a pair of rifles, then climbing onto the roof himself.

The silence held, desperately, and heeding the warning that was coming over him Britt started up the hill. Two more men climbed out of the land office window, then in the same manner, crept armed up the roof slope to crouch behind the gable. They were watching the bank, their rifles at ready.

Three armed men emerged from the General Store ahead of Britt, running quickly from the concealment of tent to wagon, approaching the perimeter of the area being sealed off surrounding the bank. Now men appeared behind the yellow pine façade of a still uncompleted saloon across the main street from the bank.

Each man was armed. Britt ran now, up through the silence of the street, reaching one of the men who had come from the General Store. The man, holding a shotgun, squatted behind the front wheel of an unhitched wagon.

Britt seized the man as he half arose to make another advance toward the bank.

"What's going on?" Britt spoke in urgent quiet.

The man hissed, "Shhh! Be quiet! That Casey wild bunch rode in just after sunup." He whispered testily, "They went into the bank." He fixed his attention on the shut door below Roody's billowing canvas banner. "We aim to break these owlhoots of robbing our bank right from the first."

"Where's Roody?" Britt asked.

"Who?"

"Roody Andrews."

The ambusher shook his head. "I don't know him."

"Hellsfire, man! The banker. He's probably in there," Britt declared. "His sister may be in there with him."

"Well, we ain't aimin' to shoot until they come out."

"If you don't know the banker, damn it, how do you know you won't be shooting him?"

"We know the Caseys. And I sure ain't going to shoot no woman!"

Britt ducked for the land office wall and ran crouching down its side.

The ambusher, in muted voice, ordered excitedly, "Come back here! Godlemighty! You'll get full of lead!"

Britt circled warily behind the land office. The bank's clapboard west wall faced him, across the street. He saw no Caseys. Britt stood up and unhurriedly crossed the street.

Thrusting from every place of concealment, behind the bank, across the street to the south, down the east hill, behind him and westward, Britt saw armament. Pistols, shotgun barrels, pointed rifles were in evidence, and the army was increasing. Britt walked slowly, hoping that the erect casualness of his approach, and his uniform, would delay the precipitation of a hail of gunfire.

He stopped behind the clapboard wall at the rear of the bank. Kneeling, he seized a foot-wide board. Bracing a foot against the sheathing, using the full strength of his legs and back, Britt heaved. The board came away so easily he almost fell.

Tacked to the studs of the flimsy structure with only shingle nails, the clapboard came free from all except the roof studding. Ducking under the wall's cross brace, Britt slid inside the small back room of the bank.

Roody stood backed against the east wall, his clothing rumpled, his arms raised high.

Dink Casey had been leaning against the rolltop desk in the center of the small room. His gun, covering Roody, swung to include Britt as he stepped inside. Through the door separating the two rooms, Britt heard one of the Caseys comment sardonically how nice "that banker feller was to leave the safe unlocked for them."

Soldier Jack Hickey's unmistakably reedy voice answered:

"The less talk and the quicker we get the hell out of here, the better off we're going to be."

The silvery clink of a bag of silver coins dropped on the floor punctuated his statement.

In calm quiet, Britt asked Roody, "Where is your sister?"

Roody, in hardly controlled hysteria, shrilled querulously, "Eve? They're robbing my bank and you want to know where Eve—"

Dink Casey cut him off. "Be quiet, banker! We aim to keep this business private." He kept moving his pointed revolver nervously from Roody to Britt, and Britt felt strong temptation to tell him that this particular bank robbery was about as private as the Chicago fire.

Instead, he adopted an apologetic tone. "I have no interest in your bank robbery," Britt said quietly. "I've got to find this man's sister," he leaned to depart through the exit of the loose board.

The gun fixed its bead on Britt's chest. "You stay put, mister. I remember you." Young Casey was moody in recollection. "You've got a bad habit of horning in whenever I'm about to score," Dink said grimly.

Britt waited until Dink's eyes made brief shift to Roody. Simply then, as if it were a routine exercise, he made a single step and kicked the gun out of Casey's hand. The heavy revolver clattered down over the lattice of the rolltop desk and thudded on the floor.

From beyond the partition Bung Casey's dull voice turned hoarse with excitement, "They're coming in the back!"

A threatening snarl of Soldier Jack's nasal voice replied, "That's fine. We'll go out the front."

Britt heard running steps around the deposit counter, the flapping of the swinging gate at the end of the counter. The front door slammed open, triggering the first volley of murderous crossfire from the townsmen surrounding the bank.

Britt yelled, "Hit the deck, Roody," and dropped flat.

Instead, Roody leaped to jerk open the door in the partition.

Dink Casey came around the desk scrambling after his gun. The roll of steady gunfire from outside riddled the planks of the frame bank. Amid flying splinters torn from the clapboards Roody staggered against the desk and dropped to the floor.

Britt saw Dink Casey struck twice, the first bullet driving him up to grab the small of his back. The second caught him in the side, wrenching him around and flinging him down in an awkward heap of wrongly bent joints and misshapen legs.

The gunfire slowly became sporadic and ceased, and became a jumble of shouting voices. Britt lay quiet on the floor, primed by caution. To move out now, into a crowd of maniacs liable to shoot down anything that moved . . . he crawled forward on his belly, listening to the approaching shouts.

When they reached the front door the yelling became hesitant, tentative, cautious. Roody, like Dink Casey, lay limp and bleeding from more than one wound. The first townsman then must have gained courage to peer inside the front of the bank, for Britt heard his shouted report that the place was empty.

Men were entering the front now, heavy footed until they stopped, their voices falling suddenly low as they became conscious of the partition and the closed door facing them. Britt heard some retreat outside with running steps.

He lay very still. The door burst inward. Britt waited. He saw boots, then cautiously approaching movement as one more reckless than the others stepped through the doorway. His shouted report, "There's more dead ones in here!" brought the mob. Dink and Roody were dragged outside. The man who grabbed Britt yelled, "This one's alive!"

It's touch and go now, Britt thought. He heard Eve's voice call out loud, outside the bank.

"That's my brother," she was whooping angrily.

The man who had grabbed Britt let go.

Britt simply stood up and followed the stampede of curious townsmen rushing outside now in curious anxiety to see everything that was going on.

Nate Richter had arrived. Through his news-gathering Richter had apparently become known to more people than any other person in Logan Station. Richter supported Eve's identification, assuring the crowd that Roody was the banker, not one of the robbers.

Richter climbed atop a wagon box, shouting, "Now is as good a time as any. We've got to elect a responsible officer. Here lies our town banker. Killed because we took the law in our own hands!"

Britt worked through the crowd toward Eve. Reverend Quigley and his wife were kneeling beside Roody. As Britt approached, Quigley, in his strongest pulpit voice, shouted, "This man isn't dead. Is there a doctor here?"

No doctor volunteered but a surly-appearing man leaning on the wagon in which Nate Richter stood announced he was a veterinary. After a cursory examination of Roody the horse doctor suggested, "This ground ain't the best place for him to be a-layin'. You ought to get him in a bed somewhere."

"He has a cot in the back of the bank," Britt said, then observed Roody's wall-eyed look of horror as his eyes skittered toward the bullet riddled frame building where he had almost lost his life.

Eve said, "We could take him down to that tent room you rented for me at the Evans Hotel."

The grocery freighter brought up his team and hooked it into the tugs of the wagon in which Richter still stood while they loaded Roody in the wagon bed. Eve climbed in to hold Roody's head. Richter sat down. With Britt, the Reverend Quigley, and his wife Cherry sitting alongside, the wagon eased downhill toward the Evans place.

Britt told Eve, "I was looking for you."

From her seat beside Eve, Cherry Quigley responded. "Eve feared I might be ill-at-ease my first night in this rough frontier camp. She came to visit me. I *was* nervous. Obadiah was making calls so late. I persuaded Eve to stay the night."

Britt instantly found himself feeling guilty. *I suspected her of mischief,* he thought, *and there she was out doing something nice for someone.* He looked at Eve now, as she sat solicitously holding her brother's head in her lap. *She can't say a kind word to Roody,* Britt thought, *but let something serious happen to him—*

Britt suspected the same of Roody. Let Eve get hurt and their endless fight would be, for that moment, forgotten. A silent wraith-like figure was walking alongside the wagon. Britt glanced up, then looked again at the figure. It was Peardeedo.

He doesn't look the same without his guitar, Britt thought.

"*El señor,*" Peardeedo asked Britt softly, "he will die? This, I think," Peardeedo added hesitantly, "it is my fault."

Britt began shaking his head but Peardeedo went on, "Last night at about three hours of the morning *la señora* Basil, me she aroused from my bed. 'Go down to the river,' she say, 'an' find the place where the brothers Casey make camp. Bring them,' she say.

"It is a long way. An' very dark. I do not find them until almost the dawn. Then I bring them. When we are here, *la señora se enoja.* With very much anger she say to these bandits, 'Where have you been? I told you I get word to you when it is time.'"

Roody stirred in the slow-moving wagon. He sat up, shaking his head. Crusted blood streaked the side of his face and fresh blood began to ooze from the wound in his temple.

Britt reached to apply pressure, pressing with his thumb to shut off the blood from the pulsing vein. "Take it easy, Roody," he urged. "We've got to find a medico to look at you—"

Nate Richter was leaning over the edge of the wagon bed. "What about Mrs. Basil, Peardeedo? Finish what you were saying."

Peardeedo shrugged. "That is all. They go away. I don't hear no more—except she said somebody is so drunk he no can find his pants with both hands—"

"That was me," Roody interrupted firmly. "Look here, I'm all right."

"Oh, hell. You're not!" Eve said tersely. "You're still leaking blood. Lie down and keep your head uphill. We've got to get that shirt and drawers off you—"

They were pulling up before the Evans tents. Richter hurdled out the side of the wagon and circled around to the tailgate to help Britt carry Roody. The surly veterinary was waiting inside the dining tent, holding a black medical satchel he had acquired somewhere along the way.

Several W.C.T.U. ladies, Mrs. Chameau and Annette among them, were stacking papers and shuffling them on the long dining table. As Britt and Nate Richter came bearing their inert burden alongside the table Mrs. Chameau was babbling, "We heard the shooting and wondered—we're preparing our first report on the church census—"

Britt and Richter stretched Roody out on the pine planks. With Roody laid out on the table Richter drew Britt aside.

"You heard our young Mexican friend," said Richter. "I'm going up to Stutz and Basil's saloon." Richter started out of the tent then turned back, pulling a newspaper out of his coat pocket as he returned to Britt. He thrust the newspaper in Britt's hand saying laconically, "First edition."

Richter left the tent. Britt fumbled with the paper, began to unfold it, and found Eve staring at him. Her eyes moved down, taking in his uniform, and she said, "Didn't Dink Casey recognize you?"

Britt nodded.

"I'm surprised he didn't shoot you."

Britt said ironically, "Dink didn't want to give away the secret the bank was being robbed."

The vet, working over Roody, stopped suddenly. He raised his head to order testily, "Everybody out!" He raised his voice more to cut through the excited chatter of Mrs. Chameau and her ladies. "There's too much racket," the crusty vet asserted. "I can't make no examination. This ain't no ladies' aid—"

The tent emptied and Britt stood with Eve near the dropped tent flap. He opened the first edition of the *Logan Station Leader* and silently read a headline, SOONERS THWARTED.

The news item was detailed coverage of the trial yesterday. It lauded Joel Decatur's defense of Eve, in proving that the town lots in contention had been staked long before the noon hour opening of the territory three days past.

> *Rascals of this ilk,* the article concluded, *are a disgrace. The* Logan Station Leader *urges them to depart in haste. This first trial in the territory was a success. Justice was done. It must continue to be done even if it is necessary to form a vigilante committee to bring such scoundrels before the court.*

Britt handed the newspaper to Eve. She read the item with no change of expression. The preacher emerged silently from the Evans' dining tent. He saw Britt and Eve standing together and came to join them.

He told Eve: "Cherry and Mrs. Evans are helping the—ah— doctor dress your brother's wounds. He has lost some blood but he still insists that he is going to be all right."

Seeing the remnants of concern in Eve's face, Obadiah Quigley added, "They are going to move Roody to a cot back in one of the tent rooms, then we can all go in."

"Where were you when the shooting started?" Britt asked the preacher.

"Cherry and I had gone to the depot," Quigley said. "A mixed train of freight and mail is in. We were expecting a crate of songbooks and several boxes of Sunday school supplies."

They stood quietly in the morning sun. Britt could hardly see how Roody could be "all right" after having seen him go down in that hail of lead. The preacher, apparently to divert Eve, kept making conversation.

"We saw some friends of yours at the depot," he told Eve. A touch of interest crossed her face and Quigley continued, "Only briefly however. The Texas Flyer makes a fuel and water stop here. Your three friends must have been hiding in the washroom. Just before the train pulled out they came running out with their suitcases and jumped aboard. It was Hampton, Nash, and Lang."

Cherry Quigley opened the dining tent flap. "You all can come in now." She led them to a tent room adjoining the dining area.

Roody sat propped up on a cot, pale and morose, but hardly appearing near death. The veterinary told Eve:

"I borrowed some carbolic the hotel lady had among her nostrums. Used some of her towels an' the water that was simmerin' on her cookstove to clean him up. He's lost blood. There's a couple furrows along his ribs an' he'll sure have to grow some new hair where that Winchester slug scalped him. But, hell, you can't kill a redheaded Irishman. I reckon he'll be all right."

Roody grumbled, "This horse doctor has played the devil with my white shirt."

"Horse doctor! Did what?" the vet sputtered. "Them's bullet holes, mister. You bled all over yourself!"

"I can patch your shirt and wash it, Roody," Eve said contritely.

Britt gazed at her in astonishment and her offer brought a surprised stare from Roody. He grinned sheepishly and said, "I heard you yell when they dragged me out, sis."

Britt suggested, "A cup of strong coffee laced with plenty of cream and sugar might buck him up a good deal now."

"I'll fix it," Eve volunteered.

"May I come in?"

Judge Trumbull's frog voice was readily identifiable even before Reverend Quigley pulled open the tent flap and assured him, "Of course, your honor."

Roody's eyes widened, startled and distinctly apprehensive.

The judge came in declaring hoarsely, "I've just come from viewing the cadavers." Trumbull harrumphed, clearing his throat.

"Banker Andrews, there's a large money shipment at the depot from Kansas City. The mail clerk doesn't know what to do with it since the bank robbery. He sent for me. Part of it is consigned to you personally, the rest to the Commercial Bank of Logan Station."

Roody groaned, "Already I had money falling out of the safe." He paused and a rising flush that improved his pallor became almost a blush of embarrassment. "Or running out the front door that is," he amended. "It was in the safe—or most of it was—" He reddened still more and small beads of sweat began forming on his forehead. To Britt he looked like a man trying to muster up courage to make some kind of a confession.

Judge Trumbull raised a plump hand, "No worrying now. I requested an Army detail. The soldiers have returned to the safe all the money the Caseys carried out. I've issued a court order. The Army will guard that bank around the clock until you're able to take over."

Still shame-faced, Roody squirmed uncomfortably on the cot. He asked in embarrassment, "I wonder if you would all step outside? Britt, you and Eve stay."

Roody began whispering while the others were still vacating the tent. He hissed nervously, "There's an empty money belt around my middle. Get five-thousand dollars from my personal funds at the depot."

Britt looked at Eve in confusion.

"What's the hurry?" Britt asked.

"All right, all right." Roody stifled angry emotion and forced himself to explain calmly, "I lost some money last night that wasn't my own. Believe me, I've learned my lesson"—he reached to take Eve's hand in contrition and pat it awkwardly—"perhaps in two ways."

With long, impatient strides Nate Richter, followed by a hurrying Joel Decatur, launched themselves well through the group waiting outside the tent room before they could be warned that Roody had asked for privacy with Britt and Eve.

The fistful of greenbacks Richter was waving helped open the passage and he was already inside, breaking into Roody's embarrassed show of affection for Eve, when Joel came following through the entrance flaps.

The impulsive newspaperman apparently sensed the strained air of privacy then, and halted, ready to apologize.

Roody almost with relief, urged, "Come in, gents. It's all right," he eased back against the pillows. "Let the rest of them come in if they want to."

Richter needed no urging. As the tent began to fill he began recounting, "Decatur took over up there. He looks to me like a qualified candidate for marshal. He's downright impressive. Threatened to get another court order from Trumbull, and an army detail to surround Stutz and Basil's tent and close them down tight. Accused them of complicity in the bank robbery. Of course they denied everything. Joel asked around the tent until he found a customer who'd watched Roody get cold-decked last night.

"This customer was a fairly tough boomer himself and said he was on the point of intervening last night while the game was going on. Basil and his wife denied that too. But our lawyer friend was convincing enough that Stutz and Basil agreed that as a show of good faith they ought to give back the money you lost. Here it is."

Weakly, Roody stripped off the money belt. In chagrined relief he handed the belt to Eve. "You know what to do with that money," he told her. With a face of wry understanding Eve took the money, inserted it in the money belt and slung it loosely across the foot of his cot.

"Judge Trumbull," Roody said, "you won't have to keep the Army guarding that bank long. I'll be there in the morning if I have to crawl on my knees all the way up the hill."

Annette Chameau said softly, "Perhaps I could help out for

a while." She glanced at her mother then looked at Britt, as if for encouragement. "I've been our church treasurer for years."

"I could sure use a cashier," Roody declared. He smiled. "And such a pretty one—"

Mrs. Chameau said stiffly, "She is an excellent bookkeeper."

"And you're an attorney?" Roody asked Joel speculatively.

"I've studied U.S. banking law," Joel said.

"Good," said Roody. "I may need a lawyer before"—he stopped thoughtfully, as if on the brink of revealing his own mischief. Then he finished vaguely: "before this is all over." Roody sighed.

"I had a small practice back in Illinois," Joel said, "but it's beginning to look like one can accomplish as much here in a few months as in an equal number of years back in older, settled parts of the country."

"My sentiments exactly," Roody confirmed. "We see eye to eye. The Commercial Bank of Logan Station is your client, counselor."

His sails are refilling, Britt thought. "I don't want to leave," he said, reaching for his pocket chronometer, "but I have"—Britt calculated—"just less than an hour before the last possible train that can get me to the West Coast in accordance with my orders. I certainly don't want to be overleave and, the fact is, I have some unfinished business here."

Britt turned to face Eve, deciding to sacrifice privacy and propriety, since this was a matter not of immediate importance, but for decision in some reasonable, and respectably distant, future time. "Eve Andrews," he said, "would you marry me?"

Eve replied offhandedly, "Of course."

Her tossed-off acceptance was unsettling. He said injudiciously, and half angrily, "You mean you would if I suggested that we get married right now?"

Eve shrugged. "You know how I hate to postpone things."

Britt was shaken. He paused to weigh his doubts, and said, "I wonder—"

Quigley interrupted hastily, "If you have less than an hour—Cherry, where is my prayer book?"

"Back at our camp, silly," his wife replied calmly.

Roody was looking at Britt in genuine awe. "At least this will solve one of my problems," he said as though astounded.

"My goodness," Quigley stammered, "the license—"

Judge Trumbull ruled in froggy hoarseness, "As yet, Reverend, this unorganized territory has made no provision for marriage licenses. There's no reason to delay the ceremony."

"But we certainly can't perform a wedding without at least a marriage certificate," Quigley mused, "and of course we must hurry. I'll tell you—let me suggest—Eve and Lieutenant Pierce will go directly to the depot. Cherry and I will meet them there. We'll hurry past our camp on the way and get the necessary document and my prayer book—we can perform the wedding at the depot."

"Fine!" Joel Decatur urged enthusiastically. "Mrs. Evans, would you be so good as to bring me Eve's telescope suitcase? I'll go get your seabag from my shelter tent, Britt. Meet you both at the depot."

Britt and Eve walked up the hill together, covering the half block to the corner before either of them spoke. At the crest, where the street turned downhill toward the depot, Britt paused. Eve's attention seemed fixed ahead, across the intersection and down the rise, where the Stutz and Basil gambling tent was open and doing business.

The Stutz and Basil emporium was prospering from the excitement that had earlier surged through the town. In the backwash of the bank robbery, the tent was busy. Its sidewalls were rolled up. Ragtime music spilled its gaudy allure temptingly out over the street.

Atop the piano, the slight form of Peardeedo was clearly silhouetted against the nooning sunlight as he swayed with the music, the outline of the guitar bulging beneath his arm.

Eve's eyes glowed. Slowing gradually, she came to a halt.

"It's just like a party," she said. "Let's go. Just for a little while."

Britt looked downhill toward the depot. The train was standing in the station.

"That train is going to pull out any minute," he said. "They only make a thirty-minute noon meal stop here."

Some mysterious intuition seemed to be reaching out from them, drawing Peardeedo, for he turned atop the piano, looking out across the short distance directly at Eve.

She drifted into the street, as though drawn by Peardeedo and the happy sounds coming from the tent. Britt again glanced downhill toward the depot.

She looked back at him over her shoulder, calling impatiently, "Britt!"

She seemed half angry, but her anger melted as she looked back toward the tent. Her eyes were all anticipation, and she took another tentative step toward the gambling tent. Britt stood, rooted.

There has to be, he thought, *an end to this. Since I first saw her in the St. Louis depot I've followed her over a thousand crazy miles. Either I keep on following her whims, or I rejoin the Navy.*

She was still moving toward the gambling tent. Britt watched the rhythm of Eve's fetching legs, the shape of her as she walked away. He was strongly drawn, but he stood, willing down the force that drew him. Then he turned downhill toward the depot.

Having turned, he did not slow his pace, or alter his course. He walked the block downhill to the depot then paused long enough to sight the conductor standing alongside the train. Britt approached him.

"How long before the train pulls out?" Britt asked.

The conductor consulted his watch. "Six minutes," he said, and turned to stroll slowly up toward the engine.

Britt went inside the depot. A small and excited group including the preacher, Joel Decatur, Cherry Quigley, and Annette Chameau awaited him there.

The chubby preacher hurried toward Britt. "We'll barely have time to recite the vows," he said restlessly. "We brought Miss Chameau as a third witness—"

"No hurry, Reverend," Britt said calmly. "It appears there won't be any marriage."

"No? No wedding?"

Britt lifted his hands emptily. "As you can see," he suggested, "no bride."

Joel was beside him now, asking, "Britt, where's Eve?"

"She stopped off at the gambling tent," Britt said.

"She stopped"—Joel scowled—"at the gambling tent?"

"The Stutz and Basil tent?" the preacher faltered.

Joel's scrutiny of Britt was somewhat accusing, as if he should not have permitted Eve to do so, and the preacher ejaculated:

"Great day! She shouldn't be in that place. We must go and get her out!"

"I'll go with you," Joel said. "I know Basil—and he knows me."

But you don't know Eve, Britt thought. *Basil isn't going to be the one who makes the problems.*

"Come, Cherry," Quigley was saying, and the first long departure whistle hooted from the direction of the engine as the preacher, his wife, and Joel hurried off.

Britt was left standing, with Annette Chameau. She watched the departing three, then turned back to Britt with a small enigmatic smile. At her feet stood Eve's telescope and Britt's seabag. Britt touched Eve's deserted luggage with a toe and said: "Would you undertake to see that her bag doesn't get lost?"

Annette nodded, regarding him mildly, her eyes calm and candid. Britt knelt to hoist his seabag. When he again stood erect she asked:

"Will you write?"

Britt balanced the seabag until it rested easily on his shoulder.

The engine's second departure hoot was short and impatient. He remembered the kiss of gratitude Annette had bestowed on him after he had rescued the W.C.T.U. delegation and led them to safety.

"Yes," he said. "I'll write."

His thought was without definite form and he stood regarding her as she regarded him. The percussive shocks of the train, unlocking its joints as it began to move, were jarring to his ears and Britt said:

"I'll start a letter when I get on the train, and mail it somewhere between here and San Francisco."

He ran then. The train was rolling and he moved briskly to catch a hand rod and swing himself up into the passenger-car vestibule. Annette must have moved briskly behind him, for when Britt flung his seabag into the space between the cars and turned to look back at the depot, she was standing almost exactly at the point from which he had leaped.

She lifted her hand, then, to wave.

Burchardt   Copy R-1

The birth of Logan Station

DATE DUE			
OC 22 '74	MAY 2 6 1982		
OC 21 '7?		JE 1 4 '85	
MR 7 '7?		OC 7 '86	
AP 11 '7?			
JE 1 3 '7?			
MY 11 '7?			
AP 1 1 '?			
JUL 2 ? 1980			
SEP 1 9 1980			
SEP 2 9 1980			
OCT 2 2 1980			
JUL 2 1 1981			